STRINGS

by

Roger Simpson

The puppet man is ancient old,

Among the strings

He has pulled and wound

His hands long lost amidst the treads

That hold the puppet man

Entwined

SUMMERLAND PUBLISHING

ISBN: 978-0-9986451-2-4

Printed in the U. S. A.
Library of Congress Number: 2017936712

Layout and Design by Pizzirani Consulting

Dedication

To the faith and love of my wife and daughter, and in memory of Howard Zinn whose voice and living example kept me afloat with his constant encouragement.

Introduction

When do you know that something has been the right deed, but for the wrong reason? The novel *Strings* answers that question. It leads from police harassment of a working-class San Francisco neighborhood to a distant, mysterious city beneath the Sahara Desert. It connects the strings between many unique characters: a powerful San Francisco politician, an ex-cop-turned-reporter and his ex-partner (a police lieutenant and Master of Zahu, the most ancient of the martial arts), and Esse, a man who comes from his desert city where advanced experimentation has evolved a science and technology far beyond the West to supposedly create a plan for world peace.

The reporter and detective are both disillusioned with day-to-day life, but their investigation of the harassment problem suddenly opens a direct line to Esse's city. His "right deed" for world peace may be for the wrong reason which might evolve into an attack against the West, city by city.

They join with a brilliant renegade scientist and Esse's only beloved daughter in a race against time to unravel the strings of power. How they get there and what they must do brings the novel into the hands of a terrorist who sees peace as the end of the West.

Prologue

Memorandum

To: Board of Trustees, British Museum
Fm. Jason Streeter, Director, Oriental Studies Section
Subject: Excavation of Wang Ny Monastery Ruins
Field Report: 2739AL
Date: December 15, 1990

I regret to inform you that the excavation at the Wang
Ny monastery ruins in Qinghai Province, China, in the
Anyemaguen Range (West) conducted from May to
October during l987 and 1988 with Dr. Ho Phe's team
from the Department of Archaeology, University of
California, Berkeley, failed to make any connections
between the fifteen granite statutes found in the cave
by the Huang (Yellow) River twelve thousand feet
below. Our hypothesis that the statues may have
originally been carved at the monastery because the
imbedded particles of clay are unique to the Wang Ny
area could not be substantiated.

In conjunction with recent diplomatic access to the
archives in Beijing, our team found drawings that
match the statues perfectly. The first twelve assume
poses that cannot be traced to any dance or ceremony
particular to the region and each is holding what
appears to be a bamboo staff that, proportionate to a
man's body, would measure fourteen inches in length
and about two inches in diameter. Their function is
unknown. The remaining three statues seem to be
incomplete. One is only complete up to the waist, like

a man kneeling in meditation, while his upper torso is yet to be carved. The second seems but the vague outline by the artist of a figure just beginning to emerge from or retreat into the stone, and the third is just a formless stone on a carved base, as if any human form had vanished.

Besides the drawings, there was little text except a reference to a "Defense of Wang Ny."   Apparently, this was an armed conflict, a battle that took place about 1200BC, but it is unclear whether it involved the monastery, the village of Wang Ny below it, or the entire province.

Finally, the excavation retrieved only what appears to be a copper ceremonial bell and fragments of cooking vessels.

Chapter One

Fall light hovered in the garden as Wo Chin watched his brothers climb the steep granite slopes behind the monastery, their robes billowing like saffron kites in the wind. Only he and the old cook remained as his brothers climbed to the Shrine of Light, a wind-sculptured cave a day's journey on the highest peak, to the annual ceremony of meditation and fasting.

Before returning to his monastic duties, the monk—just a boy of eighteen—watched longingly as the final robe disappeared beyond the last overhang. He loved the pilgrimage and had been left in charge, the youngest to practice for 12th Circle Mastery. Who was he to lead, he wondered? The winter cabbages? The last summer flowers?

Shadows now covered the courtyard of the garden as he pulled small weeds among the new sprouts. Twice he thought he had heard a cry, perhaps someone shouting or even screaming down in the village of Wang Ny. Normally there was only the wind's sigh. Yet when it shifted, he could sometimes hear the sounds of the village. Perhaps someone was being scolded or punished.

Beijing Archives, from The Defense of Wang Ny

Designate 8

The American known as *Designate 8* could feel the twitch begin. First it was a tremor, and then his lips involuntary jerked, spreading upward across his cheek and forcing his left eye into an unnatural wink. He must stop it before reaching the destination.

But there was nothing, absolutely God-forsaken nothing, to mark off the road, a black twisting mirage with a thousand miles of moon-swept sand on either side. "Guide me, Father. Please," he prayed. Nothing. Not a dune or palm since the village: a few ragged huts and a single voice chanting on the light breeze of night as his urine spattered the sand with a terrible echo in the vastness.

"Worse than the moon," he whispered, holding the edge of the seat.

Designate 8 glanced furtively towards the front seat where beyond the glass divider the driver watched the road, and Rasheed, the escort, was slumped over asleep. Rasheed had asked politely for his wristwatch. But he hadn't volunteered the quarter thin railroad digital as smooth as a white-gold stone now in his palm. Two hours beyond the village, which made it almost five since they came for him at the hotel at ten-thirty.

All his adult life he'd felt incomplete without a watch.

Shifting back and forth uncomfortably in the oatmeal colored robe they'd given him to wear over his cream-colored linen suit, he lifted the hood and felt a deeper heat as it settled on his head, pressing against his heavy jowls. He began to sweat, the hood hiding the deep and endless vacuum of night.

After the twitch began, his breath was shallower. He opened the portable bar. It was bare but for a crystal jug of water and his dented flask, carried thirty-five years since Saturday football games at the university. A long drink from the flask slowed and deepened his breathing.

If there was only something to grasp—even a twig in the barren sand.

Closing his eyes, he groped in the darkness. He searched his imagination for a landscape from his San Francisco home thousands of miles away beyond this dense compartment speeding into what appeared to be a seamless void. He pictured his favorite view from Mount Noe where the last stand of Monterey pines and ancient cypress stood in the inner city. The mountain, a hill really, he thought, broke clear of the wooden Victorian houses clustered tightly against each other along the rows of elderly, terraced streets that climbed up from south of Market and rolled around the hill to the other side and down into the Mission District. It was still a neighborhood of working people: Mexican, Irish Catholic, Oriental and Black. Secret rites of childhood had been performed beneath those trees with his gang of friends as they'd grown up in the next to last row of houses before the steep climb to the high brush, grass and trees. From up there, the view stretched down to the Embarcadero and across to Oakland and the East Bay, and then shifted to the Financial District and out along the docks toward the green curve of the Presidio and the Golden Gate Bridge. The car's gentle shift caused his hands to grasp the seat tightly, but his eyes remained closed in the shelter and coolness of the trees.

"We are approaching, sir." Rasheed's voice through the intercom startled him.

His daydream suddenly vanished as he returned to the white Bentley which was now moving directly through the sand away from the road. In front of them, silhouetted by stars, dunes rose gently from the landscape. The sand blew up over the windows with a strange whirring sound from beneath.

Rasheed pointed toward the silver hood ornament. "A road beneath," he exclaimed, almost with glee, as if revealing a prank.

Designate 8 understood. The sand was being sucked away, by what force he had no idea, revealing a cement slab heading straight at the dunes. He turned and strained to look behind, watching the sand again covering the road behind them.

The moon had passed beyond the dunes which engulfed the car like the robes of a hooded figure. He closed his eyes again, trying desperately to find himself on Mount Noe as a boy.

"Now!"

Rasheed's single word forced his eyes open and he gasped; not a hundred yards ahead there appeared to be a light through the churning sand. The closer they came the more he grasped for that hill of childhood, that place of memory and sanity. He shifted his thoughts to the one place in the city where he could sit in the grass and sort out his public life of politics, wealth and power.

The light had become a corridor, an entrance into the dune. His right hand lunged for the door handle. It was surprisingly cold and unmoving. This could well be the single most important meeting in a public life of important moments. From nowhere, a wave of almost physical guilt shot through him as the car entered the dune. What am I doing?

It was then that he realized that the twitch had stopped. He imagined the calm of the moon and the silence beyond the dune. Will this contract bring the earth to rest, to a peace it has never known? This meeting was a beginning, but why did he feel the guilt, like a son betraying a father's trust?

"Here you meet the Holy One again." Rasheed opened the door with a solemn smile, and Designate 8 slowly stepped through a thin mist of sand into a sterile unknown light.

Once inside the Holy City, they had left the car and were walking down a high, wide, white corridor. Designate 8 felt like he was sweating from every pore.

"You will bathe and wear only a robe like those around us," Rasheed said. Other robed figures crossed their path at junctions with other corridors. The faces were dark and hooded, and yet they smiled in passing.

The sweat was in his eyes, almost blurring his vision. Where were the doors in these smooth white walls? He prayed for God's guidance and a place just to be alone for a while and get his bearings. And why did he feel so frightened when he had come as an honored guest to learn the next details of his mission?

He nearly jumped as Rasheed's fingers on his arm stopped their progress. He let Rasheed turn him. They were facing what appeared to be an empty wall. Rasheed smiled knowingly as part of the wall silently slid away. Before him was a room that threatened his equilibrium even more.

There was a dark walnut bookcase with leaded glass doors along the right wall next to a small wet bar and liquor cabinet. A wide red leather reading chair, reading lamp and table stood near the end of the wall. These were perpendicular to a wall of glass framed in dark walnut with a deep window seat. His eyes momentarily repelled in disbelief from what he saw through the window. He averted his gaze to see the two sofas in green and brown tweed patterns facing a

Danish cherry wood coffee table in front of a fieldstone hearth and empty fireplace on the opposite wall. His eyes slowly, reluctantly, returned to the window. It was his own cherished view nearing twilight with yellow and pink light against the orange steel of Golden Gate Bridge, the bay in deep navy blue and the Marin hills distantly cast in gathering grey fog. It was his living room on Russian Hill thousands of miles away.

"How?"

"The Holy One has many tricks," Rasheed acknowledged. "Quite beautiful, is it not, sir?"

"Yes. Just like somebody took a picture from inside…."

"Through there you will find your bedroom and bath. There are no other rooms and we couldn't bring your cherished books, but the television gives you all the stations from your home and the bar is stocked. It's the best we can offer in this holy place"

"I'm more than grateful." He did not understand the use of "holy" but imagined it referred to wherever they were, a whole city—underground? He didn't ask Rasheed.

"Your servant's name is Dama. She will bring you whatever you wish, even one of your cheeseburgers if you desire." Rasheed laughed. "She will even entertain you if you wish." His wide grin displayed a gold front tooth, but then his face suddenly hardened, as if daring the Designate to test that last service. "Dial '1' on the telephone and she will appear. But now, bathe, have a whiskey, listen to some of your favorite music and when you are ready, eat. You need time to sleep, to let the skin catch up with your bones. After you have rested, we will take the next step."

"You know I must return to San Francisco by Friday?"

"Yes, we will watch the days and you will arrive home on time. Now, please, rest as our guest." Rasheed bowed and walked out, the wall closing behind him.

The moment he was alone, Designate 8 did as he always did after a long, difficult day at the office. He stripped to his white boxer shorts. Only now he did so with a vengeance, tugging and pulling until the cloak, his clothes, shoes and socks were a jumbled pile at his feet. A normally meticulous man, he would have immediately picked up the mess. Instead, he stepped out of it and wiggled his toes on the cool parquet entry floor, rubbing and scratching himself as the air-conditioning cleared his sinuses and he began to relax.

Then he tensed up, wondering if there were hidden cameras. "Ah, a screwin' that," he said aloud and strode across the thick burgundy carpet to the bar, poured himself a Cutty over ice, twirled and downed it in one swallow. "You're a damned scotch," he complimented the crystal decanter. Walking slowly around, he examined the room in more detail. The only thing missing were the pictures of his kids and wife on the table by his leather chair.

In the bedroom, another photo of him and his wife at a gala event five years ago, was also missing. So, they weren't perfect. But damned close. Then he noticed the drawn curtains and on impulse drew them open. There too was the exact angle of the view as seen from his living room. What were Esse's *tricks*? Some kind of laser lights?

The sun was setting into the Pacific now and lights were coming on across the city. Probably 5:30 or 6 pm, rush hour. He shuddered as the drapes closed. He began to sweat again. Had he brought all the right information? He carried his uncertainty with another large scotch into a hot bath followed by a long cool shower. When he returned to the leather chair, darkness had swept across the landscape beyond his window.

He remembered when Rasheed had appeared unannounced at his door a week before and told him nothing but that his presence was requested for a progress report, the first time he'd been summoned away from the city. Designate 8 had long been accustomed to power, but now a power far greater than he dared imagine was summoning him, a power in the form of a single man whom he'd met but once twenty-five miles off Cape Mendocino where he'd been flown by helicopter.

It had been three years ago at the height of his despondency and bitterness over the mental death of his wife in a body that still functioned. He was convinced that the world had killed her mind. It was a world full of pettiness, its fools in politics and government, its empty hypocrites in religion, its United Nations organizations whose intensions always clogged and fell away into a void of bickering. All of it a sham, all interacting to create more sparks, more tensions to assure that someday a technical-chemical holocaust would come with sunrise. Martha had died inside from such worries, trying to take and hold them all, fearing for her life and his, their children, all the children. All her volunteer work had come to nothing; the planet continued to die; there was no singular peace.

Roughly, he brushed away the tears. Nobody would ever convince him that she was mentally ill, and worse, that she should be locked away from him for her own safety. Nobody, not even his son and daughter whom he had loathed in that moment, even for that moment rejected their love, letting it be consumed by his bitterness and anger and his sense of utter helplessness. And what an irony that was; helpless yet holding power over so many. Yet in the end he had conceded.

His feelings never left him, and his sudden reclusiveness had begun to jeopardize the financial side of his life. His social calendar became as empty as an abandoned house. Without her by his side, there was no success to share.

One night in the fourth month of his sorrow when he was sitting in the window seat with his scotch watching the early evening sky, Rasheed appeared at his door. He just gave him the cassette, saying, "The man who speaks here shares your concern, your wife's concern for the planet and its rapidly declining physical, spiritual and moral standards. Listen, he offers solutions. I will return tomorrow at this same time."

A week later, the meeting off Cape Mendocino had taken place. When Designate 8 had flown away from the yacht, he was sure that the dark, frail man who came seemingly unbidden into his life had the means to create a peace that would not only stop the madness but sustain the planet. Esse had asked him to become a *Designate*, an important part of the great plan.

Now they were meeting again so he could report the activities in his area of responsibility, *Sector 1*. This encompassed the western United States from the Rockies to the Pacific, Mexico to Canada, where the first implementations would occur.

He was wondering how many others there were like himself when he abruptly jumped up. Jesus, he'd left the briefcase in the car! How could he get it? His eyes darted over the wall but his groping hands found no trace of an opening. Snatching up the phone, he quickly dialed '1.' He'd hardly poured this third scotch when the wall opened and a tall hooded figure entered, the wall silently closing behind them.

It was a woman, and she held the briefcase. She extended it to him and then clasped her hands together in the traditional eastern greeting. "I did not want to disturb you, sir. No one has touched the contents."

"Yes, ah…thank you. You are Dama?"

"I am." Her arms rose gracefully and she let the hood fall silently to her shoulders. Her coal black hair fell in thick, natural waves across her shoulders, and her aristocratic bearing and beauty brought his glass to his mouth to cover his feeling of awkwardness even though she was thirty years younger.

He'd had a thousand chances to cheat on his wife but never with someone this beautiful: olive skin, high forehead, deeply set dark eyes and soft but classical high cheek bones. Would she really *entertain* him? He wanted desperately to test that, but Rasheed's look stopped him. "Is there anything you desire?"

Designate 8 took another long swallow from the drink and laughed. "Can I actually get an American cheeseburger and french fries, with a small salad?"

She nodded and smiled. Again, her palms came together as if in prayer, and the wall opened silently again as she backed out. "I will return soon with your dinner."

Sitting back down in the leather chair, he opened the briefcase. Everything was in order. He wondered if Esse would be pleased, again fearing that the contents would be insufficient.

Yee Chin and John Lee Koshima

Back in San Francisco, October's mid-morning sun had begun to warm the crisp, intermittent breeze, and deep in Chinatown, Ming-u's Butcher Shop was sold out of its famous shrimp curry while a 150 honey ducks had already gone out for delivery in wealthy Sea Cliff and Pacific Heights. The moisture was drying in the crippled alleys and on the ancient, tarnished, red brick and stone buildings.

There was a man about six feet tall walking with an easy gait down Washington toward Grant Avenue. The fingers of his left hand gently turned a short, thick length of bamboo over and over. It was difficult to tell whether he was Anglo, mixed Chinese or Japanese, but his dress was western, a navy-blue turtle neck sweater and corduroy slacks and a camel's hair sport coat. Though he ignored the perfect day before him, there was nothing his senses missed, from the rumbling of a garbage truck passing to the soft rasp of a piece of tissue paper pushing along the gutter in the breeze.

He stopped his fingers and held the staff. The day Yee Chin had given it to him after twenty years of practice remained clear even with the passing of another decade. When he'd begun at the age of six, there was no staff, just an empty hand pretending there was, as he slowly learned the movements and meditations of the first Circles of Zahu mastery. At sixteen, he received his first practice staff of pine, but not bamboo like the one he carried now.

Yee Chin was the first and last master to bring the art of Zahu from the mountain village of Wang Ny just ahead of the Chinese Communist shadow over the Himalayas. There had been students before Jon Lee, and each day the Kiwan echoed with the sound of bare feet on the plank flooring. But down all the years, Jon Lee was the only one to receive a bamboo staff. Yee Chin had said quietly, "Neither darkness nor the sea crushes the invisible. Waves rise, fall, die and are reborn, but there is always the water. Can you carry this bamboo, Jon Lee?" He turned west toward Jackson and the North Beach District and stopped momentarily. Tourists, merchants and shoppers passed and he felt the ever-present anguish of that question and his separation from Yee Chin.

It was a year ago today that he had sat with him on the polished, redwood deck overlooking the rock garden and Koi pond at the rear of the Kiwan where Chin's quarters were. Until receiving the staff, it had been Jon Lee's daily duty before practice after school and college to rake the sand, maintaining its wave-like patterns around the rocks that lay like an unmapped archipelago.

"You've found the Twelve Circles of Mastery, Jon Lee, but we know that true mastery lies in that skill beyond just practice. Kneel, like the emerging half figure of the statue, as you seek the Thirteenth Circle of Mastery. You have all the physical skill. Few have come so far and fewer have continued onward." Yee Chin had risen gracefully from his cross-legged posture, and Jon Lee followed in silence as they walked down the wide hall to the double front doors.

There, he turned and tapped Jon Lee's right shoulder with his own staff. "A Twelfth Circle Master can crush granite in the closing of his hand, kill with a single blow, stand against an army unnumbered and give aid and comfort to anyone crossing his path, friend or foe.

"Now you leave me to live alone in the world as if I and this Kiwan had vanished. Then return in one year. Now comes the time of the true warrior, Jon Lee, living as if on your knees, living with humility and compassion in the world where you may discover the Thirteenth Circle, the first circle of true understanding." He gently touched his bamboo staff to Jon Lee's heart. "Don't let the combat you now enter devour you, my friend."

Jon Lee had stood outside in stunned silence for several moments. To him, he had now left his second home after thirty years. He could visit his mother and the grave of his father. He could continue his daily practice at Ocean Beach. Nothing really had changed beyond those walls. He was still the youngest homicide lieutenant in the San Francisco Police Department, but for the first time he felt totally alone.

He stood now in silence at Grant and Jackson. The year had truly been the most difficult combat he could have ever imagined. And trying to kneel with compassion through each day had become more distant than seeing compassion's ghost wave from the furthest shore of a fog bound lake.

The bizarre horror of homicide was there before him each day. The unrelenting violence of the world compacted into severed limbs and heads, eyes cut out and stab wounds so numerous that the victim sometimes, as his captain had once remarked, "looked like a flank steak still on the cow."

One very early morning when he sat on his deck on Telegraph Hill watching the first purple hints of dawn across the bay, the phone called him to a warehouse south of Market Street where the bloated shape of a fifty-something male in a business suit, as if neatly dressed for work, hung by a hook in his neck to a second floor brick wall, his eyes wide open and staring towards the Marin Hills and Sausalito. Jon Lee had taken the next day off and slowly drank a fifth of Jack Daniels, but the picture wouldn't leave him.

Dumb and blind to the world, just as he had felt this year as if all the purpose had been sucked from him. His job had become routine and meaningless. He'd split up with the woman he thought might be his wife. It had all become this unending blend of mindless incidents, and he was becoming like the man staring at the bay, cold and silent under its weight.

Getting his MA in Criminology from Berkeley during his second year at the department had filled him with a passion for justice. But it seemed that now even the perfect arrest and evidence would be shredded and someone would be out there another day to maim and murder. As he stood there, hesitating to cross the street, he felt as if he'd lost any sense of compassion and was taking on the sinister and cynical qualities of those he pursued.

Glancing in the window of a Chinese gift shop, his reflection didn't look like a drunk, and he'd never, however bad he was hung over, missed a day of practice. There on the misty shore beyond Golden Gate Park, he relived each day the *Defense of Wang Ny* as he blocked, twirling through the fog, striking with the bamboo staff, fending off an enemy without number. Yet even the practice seemed frantically futile, a counterbalance to the nights on his deck where he sat late among his Bonsai pines, cedars and cypresses drinking Jack Daniels as the light ended in the west and he faded into sleep.

23

Jasmine incense clung to the cool stillness of the Kiwan's double-doored entry. He felt the continuous sense of harmony there, but also felt what he had never felt before: fear. He could not move from the black slate tile of the entry onto the dark wood plank flooring that led to the practice room, temple and Yee Chin's quarters. At last, Jon Lee stepped forward, but before he'd taken three steps the robed figure, more shadow than man, stood suddenly in the passage.

Jon Lee bowed and it was returned. Through the dim light, he could not clearly see the ancient smoothness of Yee Chin's face. The older man raised his bamboo staff. In size, it was the same as the one Jon Lee held, but Chin's had the deep darkness and pearl smoothness of use and age. It was far older than the man. In spirit, it was in the line of masters beginning with Wo Chin in the mountain monastery. Yee Chin placed it across his chest. The gesture symbolized a decision without doubt or a second thought.

"One year to this day has passed."

"I wasn't worthy of showing up today, Master." Jon Lee let his shoulders fall.

"You're still the warrior, my friend. You can't lose heart in combat."

"I feel overwhelmed by the world out there. I...I've lost heart."

"Do you think you're the first 12th Circle Master to feel this way?" Yee Chin reached out with his free hand and touched Jon Lee's arm.

"But this is my world. Out there is a world of tragedy and darkness, a world that seems more filled with evil every day. Please, let me come back and teach again. At least then it would be easier to face that." He motioned toward the hand carved front door. "Let me enter again."

The faint edge of a smile crossed Yee Chin's lips, but it was touched with empathy. "What do you think it was like for me. I cried and moaned and got drunk, just like you. As others probably did before us. You have entered the 13th Circle of Mastery and there's no turning back. You know that. Besides the physical warrior, I also see the spirit in your eyes." Yee Chin bowed again. "Don't lose heart in this combat, Jon Lee. For thirty years, you have prepared for it. Don't lose heart. Return when the combat with this world dies in you."

Jon Lee wanted to protest, but instead he bowed, backing down the hall. When the door closed, Yee Chin appeared to slump imperceptibly. He turned and walked to the temple. There he would light three candles for his student: one to light the road in the world, one to light the road within and the last to keep the others burning.

San Francisco Police Mc Grady, Capt. Morrison, Powerful Developer, John Locke

As Jon Lee walked numbly out the Kiwan door, across town Chief McGrady emerged painfully from his staff car in front of police headquarters. His gut ached from too much rich food and booze. He had been the lunch speaker at the University Club where he'd talked *law and order*, keeping prisons tough and bringing back the death penalty as the only meaningful deterrent to crime. Same old crappola, he thought, letting out a belch loud enough to echo off the glass and grey granite building. The university types were all liberal jerks anyway.

"Weak bastard!" he mumbled, forever promising himself to eat salad next time, and no booze. "Go to the gym" he admonished, knowing he probably wouldn't. He smirked at the building. *Worthless piece of crap* because it was practically pinned against the freeway so his office view was speeding cars and a minute and distant glimpse of the Golden Gate Bridge towers.

McGrady lacked the two prerequisites of any politician: he wasn't a social cop and he'd never learn to bullshit. He knew it, and he knew that at fifty-six he'd never grow into them. So, he consistently took a beating from the press and city hall. Thus, his life as the chief wasn't the romance he'd dreamed about as a walking beat cop downtown, directing rush hour traffic, working bunko, robbery and, finally, homicide as he rose through the ranks.

Now he saw the romance as just a series of what he called *drudges*. He was always having to drudge here and there for purposes so empty and off target from being a working cop, where you weren't admired for talking theatre and art but for handling yourself and your people against some sick bastard with a knife or gun.

Still, McGrady had no illusions. He knew he was still a street cop with misguided ambitions, and he wanted out badly. Like everybody else, he had two kids in fancy Ivy League colleges and a wife who spent like they had real money. Riding up the elevator, he wondered how San Francisco's premier and somewhat shady developer, Charles Locke, knew that too, and began expanding their relationship from a social acquaintance to the offer that could have landed Locke in jail.

Coming in the rear door of his office to avoid his secretary, he went straight to the private bathroom and popped a couple of Maalox, splashing cold water on his face. That and opening his belt and unbuttoning his pants to let his belly roll free revived him, and he blinked as if he'd never seen the room full of dark brown leather chairs and a couch, except for a conference table and his desk.

Outside, the cars never stopped zipping by. He imagined the wall to his west wasn't there. The soft green hills of Marin County came into his imagined view and moved further north into the wine country where he had his eye on a two-hundred-acre vineyard with a great old stone and wood farmhouse right in the middle, surrounded by rolling hills and blue sky. Then, no more blood pressure, jackass politicians and bleeding hearts.

He recalled his Syrian grocer from his rookie days who'd told him that a thief in his country lost a finger or a hand, and rapists and murders hung in village squares within a week. Sure, it was primitive. But it worked, crime and quick punishment.

San Francisco would never see that. A deep bitterness for the system was about to overcome him, but he forced himself to shuffle through the messages, hoping there wouldn't be one from Locke. Of course, with his luck, there it was atop the pile, "Charles Locke, 12:15 p.m. Please call immediately."

McGrady's stomach churned. Locke wanted to know if the plan he and McGrady had constructed so carefully and quietly was ready to go tonight.

Suddenly he thought he would puke and stumbled into the bathroom. False alarm. As he pushed himself up from the toilet bowl, he glimpsed the thin black hair combed across his skull like a loose pile of seaweed. His slightly bloodshot, red-rimmed eyes watched his fingers poke the pinkish white flesh along his cheeks which shuddered.

"Blue Operation," they called it. So quiet that only the Special Intelligence Division's (SID) Captain Morrison knew. Six million, Locke had offered. A vineyard and retirement and plenty left over. No more of what police work had become: disrespect for the law and a bunch of spics, niggers, fags and their screaming Jew liberal lawyers and supporters turning cops into political punching bags. Real police work had died. He felt barely a hint of guilt for getting out like this.

But why the Malloy District? The old neighborhood where he and lots of guys he knew like his sometimes friend and enemy, the mayor, Joe Hennessy, had grown up. It was all old Victorians that were now being restored by fags and white collar people because the price was still right. He'd briefed Joe on it, who didn't like the idea one bit. But McGrady had convinced him with the phony story he and Locke had made up. McGrady hoped that his SID could pull it off without too much press.

Sometimes during these past weeks, he'd wished that it would somehow come unhinged. He couldn't stall anymore. It was scheduled for 1830 hours tonight, and Morrison had to brief his people in a few hours. Should have called him yesterday.

McGrady grabbed the phone and punched out Morrison's extension. All this shit for a little clump of

29

maybe worthless real estate up there on Mt. Noe. Up beyond the houses you couldn't even build, but Locke said his "Corfu Village" condos would leave that green space. Why wouldn't these people sell? The offer was huge. He couldn't figure how Locke stood to make a dime. Four beat up Victorians, and if "Blue" didn't come off smooth, he could risk alienating the whole neighborhood. Why there, why not do the project out in the Haight and help get rid of the few hippies still hanging around since the sixties? Christ, way over twenty years and they were still there.

But he knew why those folks up on Mt. Noe didn't want to sell. It was like giving blood. Roots and family ties. Well, at least it looked like one of them would sell—the plumber.

But what was Locke up to? Why did he insist that his backers said that had to be the exact place? Were they thinking of turning the neighborhood upscale and into what was happening throughout the city, an influx of those dot.com Nazis who were pushing old timers out as prices rose? He started feeling sick as he waited for Morrison to answer.

Chapter Two

Wang Ny was a small village, maybe two hundred people, yet its renown had reached far down the great Huang River to its mouth at the port city, where the craftsmen of Wang Ny carried their beautiful handwork of gold and silver to be traded and sold. The boy went to the village only when it was his turn to beg. The name of the distant port city was unknown to him. Another row of cabbage was almost weeded when the cook came hobbling across the stone courtyard followed by a farmer whose eyes were wide with terror.

As he gasped for breath, the villager bought the earlier screams to life. The village below Wang Ny, about a two-hour descent, had been attacked and burned, the women defiled, the men tortured and killed by a marauding warlord and his followers. They had already begun the climb to Wang Ny, holding the heads of every member of the region's ruling family on poles as they came. But what was to be done, the villager asked? Few had heard of the power of Zahu, and now in the villagers' hour of greatest need the monks, sworn to consecrate and defend life, were gone. "Nothing, nothing but you, a boy!" the man stammered almost hysterically, "and...this old one. We fed and clothed you, all of you. Where are you now to help and protect us?

31

Four hours after McGrady called Morrison, night was settling in through a long yellow winter sunset as the gathering white mists became fog across the seven hills of San Francisco. It muffled the metallic whine of an engine starting up in the SID parking lot. The black Ford sedan, sterile and unmarked, moved slowly like an old cripple to the ramp and stairs below double doors lettered "Special Intelligence Division, SFPD."

Sgt. Willy Joseph killed the engine and lit a cigarette. Smoke curled out the half-opened window while he tapped the steering wheel with thumb and little finger, beating out an erratic rhythm. Though he looked like a pug, he'd only lasted in the ring eight months as a pro, but left with the defeated face of a veteran. His nose and one ear were squashed and his jaw seemed permanently slammed up against his lips, giving him the look of a surprised frog.

"Come on, asshole," he whispered irritably, staring at the double doors. As he raised the cigarette, it clipped the steering wheel and the glowing coal broke off, falling like a dead star onto the rumbled, green, polyester sports coat. "Jeeezus!" He batted it with his free hand, but too late. Yet another pin hole had appeared, this time on the right pocket.

"Morgan, where the hell are you?" he called toward the closed window of the passenger's side. The double doors remained unmoved. Willy shook his head and lit the stub. The inhale calmed him a little.

Glancing into the misty night, he tried to figure if he had everything straight from Morrison's surprise briefing an hour earlier. Willy had drawn the *Blue Operation*. It never had a name until tonight, but somehow it tied in with the last few months when SID started leaning on the Malloy District with a lot of chicken shit parking tickets that had escalated into giving the gays a hard time on the street, like checking I.D.s. None of it made any sense.

After twenty-four years, he knew how to lock step through details good and bad, but this one was eating at him. He kept figuring he'd learn more, but there was nothing. Just rumors, and all crazy, like Morrison's briefing tonight that the mob was moving in and drugs were on the rise because of the long exodus from the Haight District to the Malloy of aging hippies and college kids.

Joseph knew they weren't deadbeats. Nothing but air, nothing to grasp, and all he'd gotten from the beat cops was that the SID was breaking their trust with the neighborhood. He glanced again for the fourth time at the double doors. "Morgan, where the shit are you, dummy?" He spit out loose tobacco and crushed the Lucky in the overflowing ash tray. Sure as hell, somebody was gonna get hurt, civilian or cop. He knew he couldn't leash the other teams on this detail any more than he could figure what locals might do. Willy lit another Lucky, steadying his hand on the wheel and bent toward the flame. He blew smoke towards the double doors, and seconds later they swooshed open to voices and radio music, dying instantly to leave only the tap-tap of Morgan's leather heels down the cement stairs.

"Hey, what kept you? In the can with the new *Playboy* or what?"

"Got a cotton swab stuck in the barrel." He tipped the shot gun forward and slammed it into the dashboard brace.

"You, cleaning a weapon?"

"Yeah. You never know on nutcase details like this."

"Morgan, this is the Malloy, not the Filmore or Hunter's Point, we're not goin' on loan to Oakland, huh?"

Morgan closed the door, the engine came up and they idled toward the exit. "Yeah, right, Willy." Both were silent for a moment as the car squealed onto the wet street and headed toward Broadway and North Beach where they would wait the call from Morrison, who, another surprise, was supervising *Operation Blue* himself.

"How'd we get so lucky?" asked Morgan.

"Bad lucky. You got your vest on?" He swung the car left through a street of warehouses south of Market.

"Come on…. vest…give me a break. You check the tires on this blimp?"

"What's this tire thing lately? That your new fetish?"

"I just don't want any flats on a night like this. I'm not crazy about bricks either. We're not exactly popular out that way."

"Tell me about it. But we drew it and we play it out. I'll buy you a pastrami up at the Chicago Deli. You can hold court on the sidewalk with all your main line buddies until we get the call." Morgan managed the hint of a smile.

"I wish it was morning, Willy. The old lady making breakfast."

Mike Hamilton, ex-cop and Pulitzer Prize winning San Francisco Chronicle Reporter

By the time they'd passed the San Francisco Chronicle building, most of the offices were dark. Up on the second floor, the only lights in the newsroom ran down the center aisle which separated local from national and world news departments. It was all desks

35

and partitions except for a small tile area by the elevators and a few glass cubicles in the rear, and it was always musty with its ornate molding and tobacco brownish ceiling. Odors of cheap and expensive perfume lingered and locked with smells of perspiration which clung to the rows of wooden and metal desks. And though most of them held an assortment of computers, a few electric typewriters remained scattered throughout the room like clacky relics of recent history. No desk lamps were on except one far off the center aisle on the local news side near a bank of high wooden windows.

Mike Hamilton had all ten fingers on the keys of a black, manual Remington upright whose enamel top was singed with cigarette burns. Mike picked up a cigarette sitting there and put it out. He paused to look at the copy. Then his fingers bounced furiously across the keys for several minutes nonstop until he abruptly pulled out the yellow sheet.

What he was writing could have been done as late as Saturday morning, but in the past year he begrudged the paper any of his weekend hours though he hardly knew what to do with them himself. He ran his thick fingers through curly, black but graying hair, his *Anglo-Afro* as he called the thick curls that reached the collar of his yellow button-down shirt. In that bleak light, he opened the top desk drawer and looked at the picture of his wife, Julie, and their two kids, Caddy and

36

Mike Jr., who smiled back at him. Before, he had spent too much time at the paper, but not as much as police work had cost him for ten years before that.

Slowly, he closed the drawer and forced himself to look at the copy. It was pathetically entitled, "Kill the Nematodes!" which was his weekly contribution to the Sunday *Home and Garden* section. He was known as "The Plant Guy," which was a nice brief diversion from his usual city hall beat.

Mike was penciling in some corrections when the elevator opened and the sound of spiked heels crossed the wood and tile floor coming toward him. He took off his steel-rimmed drugstore glasses, a fallout from his very early flower child days, and watched a short, slightly stout but attractive woman silhouetted by the lobby's neon set down a suitcase and come down his aisle. He got up and hugged her. They saw each other every day at press briefings for the mayor's office.

Sue Obern had left the *Chronicle* a year before as an aggressive young reporter to join the mayor's staff as Press Secretary under his Chief of Staff, Vice-Mayor Shelia Vernin. Sue wasn't pretty like Julie with her long red hair and athletic body. Very respectfully, he thought of Sue as a bull terrier with great legs and a cynicism to match even Mike's.

"Ah, the plant man. Caught ya." She kissed his cheek.

37

"At what Obern…I'm innocent. Just picking nematodes out of your strawberry patch."

"Gross. But I figured you'd still be hanging around here."

"You know you'll have to laugh at all my bad jokes and puns." Mike pulled up the wooden chair next to his desk and patted the seat. "Sit a spell, cowgirl. Tell me what's up while I buy you a drink." He pulled out a pint of vodka and two Styrofoam cups and poured, handing one to her.

"Thanks." She sipped. "Tell me, do all you Pulitzer men have this little class?"

"Some of us old timers literally teem with little class."

"Two years."

"Old, old, old news. Come on, tell me about it."

She crossed her legs which brought the skirt half way up her thigh. "Just needed a moment of sanity before Berkeley. An invite from my sister and her hubby, and yet another blind date with the newest associate professor in the English Department."

"Give them credit for at least trying, Obern." He paused to study her face. "But there's more, right? Problems at city hall?"

"Naw. Shelia's a bitch sometimes but the mayor's always a sweet guy. Incredible patience. Frankly, I don't know how he puts up with her."

"He seemed edgy at the briefing for this new Embarcadero Project."

She smiled and squinted. "Only you would notice, Pulitzer man. You catch all the chinks."

He downed his drink and poured another. "What good are prizes?" He shook his head and spoke with a tinge of bitterness. "Fight the forces of evil. How trusting and romantic I was." They were silent for a moment. "What am I doing? We're talking about you. Maybe the bloom's off the new job?"

She shrugged. "Maybe. Maybe it's just turning thirty in a little apartment on Nob Hill."

"Cosmo faces reality?" She hit his arm. "Your birthday is next week, Tuesday. You're having dinner with me. You name the place."

She laughed lightly and stood, draining her cup. "Thank you. Okay, I'm ready for the new guy in English. Walk me out?"

Going back up the aisle, Mike sailed his copy onto another desk and they rode the empty elevator down. "Mike, how are your weekends? If you don't mind…."

"You know. Clean and sew, tend my vegetable garden on the roof mostly. Errands. Anna has me down to dinner." He smiled teasingly at her. "While you seduce frightened young English professors."

The doors opened onto the high marble columned lobby. "We heart people don't always get on well with those head people, but tell that to my brother-in-law." Most of the chandeliers had been turned off, and the evening news echoed around the lobby's dome from a portable TV on the desk by the front door where the security guard sat. They walked slowly toward him. "You...you must miss...the house."

Mike watched the fog pressing along the high windows and heavy glass doors of the lobby. "The Malloy's an okay neighborhood: cheap restaurants, best weather in the city, friendly folk. I can see practically the whole city from the roof, and Anna being Jon Lee's mom and my landlord, and sometime my Mom too, it's kind of like I'm family there. He and his brother Naga are always dropping in for dinner. If I want to go back to nature, I cross the street, go through a friendly old Russian's backyard and climb the hill. Presto, ancient trees atop Mt. Noe. What else can there be when you hit forty plus?"

"How about companionship?" She stopped.

He laughed and opened the doors. They stood on the top step looking down into a red brick plaza that led through its rows of trees and benches to the fading rush hour traffic. A faint hint of purple and orange light reflected high up off a distant office building. Mike stared momentarily at the light. "Companionship? Yeah, maybe, Sue." His vision shifted downward to the street lights. "Hell, another down and dirty Friday night. Come on, I'll walk you to the BART."

As they crossed the nearly empty plaza, Sue put her arm in his and they began to slowly sway through the leaves a breeze had stirred. "What do you think of this condo project going up across from you?"

"A what?"

"Yes."

"Replace those old beat up Victorians. You're kidding."

"Twenty-fourth, off Castro? Your street, correct?"

"Nobody has said a thing to me. I can't believe the Russian, the retired plumber, a gay couple or the hippie couple doing the restore would even consider selling.

"It would only take three houses to make it work; the one closest to Castro Street is already sold. I saw the plans on Shelia's desk on Wednesday."

"Those houses are the plumber, the Russian, the gays and the leather smith, in that order. But why would Shelia, the vice mayor, have the plans? That's the planning commission and supervisors' job, right?"

"Natch. But she was really sweet-talking the major about this. It's *Windhover Construction*." A strong breeze was coming up Market from the Ferry Building.

Mike nodded with a half-smile, as if he understood completely. "Figures, the infamous but socially prominent Charles Locke, with his connections."

"That's the guy, but I don't know about the infamous part."

"Believe it, Sue, a dirty finger in every pie in town, practically. When I was working on the drug story, his name came up more than once in relation to organized crime, but I could never make any connections. What do you think Shelia is doing?"

"Come on, Mike, we both know that one. Political ambitions. Big time. She wants to be mayor when Joe Hennessy retires. And even though the mayor's honest, Locke's a big financial donor. Got one house already. Guy named Twain or Thween."

"The plumber, little Homer. Use to be a ward boss out there, small time politics." Mike shook his head. "Anna's gonna be really upset. Think of the mess, all the new traffic. What does it look like?"

"A terraced Greek island village. Looks too expensive for the neighborhood and way out of place." They reached the BART entrance.

"I think the mayor grew up around there somewhere."

"He loves the Malloy but he's also progressive. Hard to tell what he'd do. He's already upset about the SID stuff going on out there. I heard him raising hell on the phone for Chief McGrady week before last."

"That's trouble I want to avoid."

"But it's your neighborhood. Gee, I remember an investigative reporter I once knew who would have jumped at that story, because the wealthy Charles Locke tie-in with our vice mayor could make it more bizarre by the minute."

Mike handed her the suitcase and kissed her cheek. "I'm not him anymore, Sue."

"So much the loss."

"Would you keep me posted on this if you hear anything, weird or not?"

"Sure."

"At your birthday dinner, you can tell me about the new man in English."

"Boring," she called back, descending the stairs.

Mike watched her until she disappeared into the tunnel, then turned and walked quickly away. Automatically, his hand went for his pocket. Feeling through his change and keys, he touched a tiny rubber ball, the kind small children play jacks with. His large hand and fingers gathered around it, holding on gently as he crossed Market to catch a trolley home.

Chapter Three

"What if the gold and silver objects you create were offered?" Wo Chin asked innocently.

The villager shook his head violently in exasperation, turning suddenly toward the gates of the monastery as if fearing the warlord's presence already upon him. "They desire our blood even more than our gold! We are powerless. But our people hid our craftsmanship now. This warlord will never have the satisfaction of finding even a single gold bracelet."
The man spit in the pile of weeds near the boy's feet.

Wo Chin started for the gate and they followed. "Go to the village and bring everyone here. Quickly"

Charles Locke withdrew his attention momentarily from the nervous ramblings of Chief McGrady's voice to watch the last of the blue, yellow and white sails returning to Tiburon Harbor. His view beyond the open French doors was to the west from a promontory of lawns and gardens rolling gently down to the private dock where his sixty-foot boat, "Windhover," swayed against her moorings.

Further to the south and distant were the gleaming orange, steel spans of the Golden Gate

Bridge. His eyes turned southeasterly. There, to his chagrin, was, as he called it, *the wart*, Angel Island. Blocking a complete view of the city, it stood like a benign tumor swarmed over daily by tourists and locals trying to find nature. But the view it impeded was insignificant compared to what he could see; the shimmering lights on the hills as they flowed down to meet the ever-darkening waters of the bay at the Embarcadero, Fisherman's Wharf and Aquatic Park.

McGrady emphasized a point, but Locke's only interest was getting the job done, not the details. Again, he drifted away from McGrady to recall the day twenty years ago when he'd acquired this land from a much older and seasoned competitor who had foolishly taken seriously that maudlin virtue, trust, and ended up on the very short end of the deal. Locke and his wife built the house and supervised the landscaping themselves.

Although the sparkle of prom night dances and school parties had vanished with the marriages of their son and three daughters, there were still the fashionable charity balls accompanied by an elite social orchestra. As summer had ended, he missed the sounds he cherished most, his grandchildren at play, drifting up from the lawn and dock or pool on long summer afternoons.

Not that he cared, but he had McGrady repeat some detail because he sensed that the urgency in his voice required affirmation. To Locke, this was just

45

another development project like so many before it that had made him wealthy. Gamesmanship, including some always questionable illegalities, had been some part of each success, but never had he found himself as liaison between the chief of police and the mayor's chief assistant on one side, and a semi-retired plumber on the other! Yet, incredibly, Thween's original phone call and its details checked out regarding the Corfu Village project. A goddamned plumber. Someone he would have employed. With his hands-on millions. It was almost eerie. The funds were in escrow. There were no flaws even though his people had double-checked everything. And he was receiving an astounding ten million as a bonus, for reasons he couldn't understand, from the Middle Eastern investors whose only stipulation was that it be built at that exact location.

McGrady whined for still more assurance as Locke examined his long fingers. "Chief, everything sounds in order. Now, leave it that way and try to relax. Call me in the morning with your report, which I trust will be positive. Goodbye." Locke hung up, admiring his hands.

They were the hands of a pianist, though his mother's dreams of private lessons had only become the meager instruction his public schools could offer. He continued to take private lessons from an elderly virtuoso with the symphony, and still played in a very average manner. Delicately, he held the phone again and dialed. It was a little more than an hour before his wife would call him to cocktails, and first he must practice.

He dialed Homer Thween's number, and it rang five times before Thween picked it up. He'd been standing naked in the bathroom, dripping from a shower, examining a small welt of unknown origin—a pimple, worse? —near the nipple of his sagging right breast. Grabbing the frayed cloth robe from its door hook, he threw it over his shoulders, still holding the towel with one hand to prop his breast up as his free hand probed momentarily at the pinkish spot until he needed to pick up the phone. As he was about to lift the receiver, the hand leaped back and Thween dropped his breast to wipe the phone hand completely dry. Though around the construction trades all his life, Homer had an unaccountable fear of electricity and still believed the story that a wet phone hand was just a step away from electrocution. Assured that his round little hand was dry, he picked up the phone. "Thween here."

"Good evening, Homer."

"Ah, Charlie. Been waiting for your news. So has the boss."

Homer had spoken hardly a dozen words and Locke was already annoyed. Since the military, no one had ever dared call him "Charlie," and Thween's reference to *the boss* grated equally on him, because for the first time in his career he had no idea who that was.

47

But he managed to restrain himself and began to relate McGrady's report.

As he listened, Homer stared at his small, chubby body in the oak framed oval upright mirror standing by the window on what had been his wife's side of the bed. He had thick shoulders, hairy and stooped, arms still heavy with loose muscle and thin, white, slightly bowed legs crosscut with blue veins. He kept grabbing for his crotch, repeating the action almost unconsciously as he interjected questions into Locke's report. It was a habit his devout Catholic wife had detested and protested against vigorously during their forty-five-year marriage. But to no avail. He'd kept at it, meaning no harm, a comforting gesture shared only with himself.

The disdain in Locke's analytical manner wasn't lost on Thween, and he relished the position fate had doled out to him in this unique situation: the plumber as king-for-a-day lording it over a man who would probably never have glanced his way had Homer and his crew ever done work for Locke's mighty Windhover Construction Company. He'd have gladly done this job for his friend just to tweak Locke's nose.

"Well then, just give me a toot when the Chief has this wrapped up. If this doesn't blow things wide open, I don't know what will." He finally managed to get into the robe but didn't tie it. "Oh, listen. I was down at them fairies' pet shop today. Bought our little

Hot Dog a new rubber ball and got a chance to sort of *feel* 'em out." He laughed hard at his pun and grabbed himself twice for good measure, but Locke didn't seem to appreciate the humor. Stuffy bastard. "You know what I mean? Me being their neighbor and I'm selling. Let me tell you, their little buns are scared shitless over the health department guy that that Shelia Vernon sent over there. What I'm saying is, let's keep on them. Forget old man Dobkovnic for the moment. Crack the fairies first, then Dobkovnic, and last, the hippie and his whore. That's how the boss wants it, one, two, three."

"I'll pass that along to McGrady." Locke's end was silent for a moment. Thween was stuck for anything else to say so he just waited, practicing various smiles in the long mirror. "Mr. Thween, Homer, I simply must have more information on the silent partner or partners. You surely understand my..."

"Charlie," Thween interrupted, "we've been over that bridge a dozen times. The A-rabs'll be coming out soon after construction gets along, and you're gonna meet them, I promise. Okay? The boss says they're good guys."

"Yes, but...."

"Come on, Charlie, you gotta be happy with what you got for now. Don't worry about the boss. I'll pass this all on to him." He hesitated for a moment, trying to concoct a way to settle Locke's curiosity once and for all. "Charlie, I'm not trying to play games here,

49

but you gotta trust the way things are. It's…well, much bigger than just us."

"What is bigger? Look, I've got to be able to talk to someone if the plans require modification."

"That won't be a problem. Look, there's a lot I don't know, so you and me are kind of in the same canoe. Me, I'm just a little guy, Charlie, a semi-retired plumber who a powerful friend came to for a favor. And I went to you 'cause you're the best at what we needed. We both gotta be patient. You got any problems, I can handle 'em with one phone call to him. Oh, and he appreciates what you're doing with McGrady."

"He's a horse's ass."

"Ain't we all to somebody, Charlie? The boss knows that. Call me tomorrow. Good night now." Homer Thween held the phone until the silence clicked to a dial tone. Finally, he set it down, closed his robe and tied the belt.

Downstairs, he waited for Senora Rosa's special frozen Mexican dinner to bake in the oven. It took only four minutes in the new microwave, but he always used the oven. The microwave had been a present from his son when cancer took Nina from him. He couldn't remember how long ago the same frozen dinner every Friday had begun against Nina's protests, which over the years had finally subsided. Maybe it began right after the Pope said meat was okay on Friday. He couldn't recollect. Anyways, she'd gone along with it, bless her heart, the two of them sitting and talking at the kitchen table, him with a beer, her with a 7-UP. They always waited until the two Senora Rosa's sizzled before them in the overhead light casting its brownish glow through a glass fixture which had for years served as the burial ground of flying creatures. In all their years together, he'd never taken it down and washed it as she'd so often asked.

Tonight, as always, Senora Rosa was delicious, and he ate the beans, beef enchiladas and rice slowly, not wanting it to end. But when it did, he'd look for a fight on TV or walk down to Moe's later after the SID got done for another beer or two.

As he ate, carrying on the same quiet two-way conversation he did every night with her empty chair, his mind keep flicking over the shadows, the black spaces of this project, the parts that worried him but without any reason. Homer trusted his friend like a brother. No doubts. But it was the others, people from places so strange he wouldn't know where on the map to look for them. Their kind of money was only as familiar to him as the evening news about the Middle East. So much to be offered just to relay information for a friendship that reached back to childhood.

At first, Homer had flatly refused the money he was supposed to get. He gulped his beer and let out a long belch. Three million. He belched again. "Excuse

51

me, Nina, I'm sorry." He didn't need that kind of money. Didn't want it. He'd saved. He was doing okay. No, this was just one for a good friend. It would leave more for the kids and he didn't really mind leaving the old neighborhood now that Nina was gone and the kids scattered from Seattle to L.A.

"I know so much more than I can let on to Locke, Nina, and it kind of scares the hell out of me. But it's right, a better life, he says, for everybody all over the world. He wouldn't ask me to do something that was wrong. He wouldn't. You know him well as I do." Homer went to the sink and washed the fork and put the dinner tray into garbage. Then, for no reason at all, his hands began to shake.

"Goddamn it, Bear…!"

Bear Danielly interrupted again. "Eight years I've run this Malloy precinct, John. They like us too. Maybe even trust us. And that took years to build. Now you come in with your damned SID and, well, by God, you're destroyin' all that. And you don't even give a man the decency of a reason!"

"I can't," Captain Morrison pleaded. "Now, listen. I…." But between the "I can't" and the "now, listen" Danielly hung up. Morrison let the receiver fall from his hand to its cradle, which it hit sideways and fell with a thump to his desk. He got up, leaving it there, and went directly through the outer office without saying a word to anyone. He had no reasons for his old friend, because he had been given none by McGrady except the bullshit story about drugs and some mob move.

In his car, he lit a short thin cigar and without opening the windows, let the cheap smoke bury him. He stared blankly at the dash. Then his eyes drifted to the rearview mirror and his thin face and butch haircut. He imagined he looked much older than forty-five. Finally, he picked up his radio mike.

Across town, Joseph and Morgan were leaning against their car eating pastramis thick with mustard on French rolls when the call came. "SID one. Leader. Tack 3."

Joseph reached through the window and got their mike, switching channels. "One, go ahead."

"Units two and three moving. 18:47 now." They checked their watches against Morrison's voice. "Commence operation, 19:15."

"One, rolling and out."

They dropped their barely eaten sandwiches in the trash, got into the car, pulling into the early North Beach Friday night. "I'll take the scenic route," Joseph said.

"Whatever, Willy, just make it the long way around. Maybe it'll be over by the time we show."

"Yeah, sure, especially with us being on point." Sgt. Joseph jammed the accelerator to make the light and the dark car flashed across the Columbus intersection and headed for the Broadway tunnel. Once through it, they cruised out Broadway into the upper Marina District.

Morgan lit a Camel, blowing the smoke towards his wind wing. "You really think there's anything to this crap from Morrison today?"

"Who knows?"

Morgan ran his hand back through his thick, greasy, brown hair and shrugged. The car swung suddenly left as Joseph gunned it up Divisidero into the trees and mansions of Pacific Heights. As they crossed Jackson Street, Sgt. Joseph noticed two little girls, probably about eight or nine, standing by the high living room window of an imposing three-story red brick house on the corner. Their blonde hair glistened in curls, and they wore identical black party dresses with lace trimmed white collars. Behind them, he saw for an instant the dancing shadows of a hearth fire on the high beam ceiling. His jaw relaxed, and leaning back in the seat he yawned and eased off the gas a little.

"Look, Morrison didn't call it; he just passed it along from the fat boy, McGrady. Let's go do it, get it done, forget it, and I'll buy you steak, eggs 'n a beer at Jerry's."

Morgan lit another Camel off the one he had going and glanced at his partner in the car's early winter darkness. "Yeah, with bar glass in our ears." He coughed out the first inhale. "It stinks, Willy. This ain't cop work."

Morgan hunched down in his seat as the car rolled off Pacific Heights and down into the Filmore District. As the ground leveled off, they were under a mesh of trolley, bus, telephone and electrical wires that hung thick along the street like the web of a prehistoric spider, tight and impenetrable against the first evening stars.

"Guy I know, used to be on the force, lives out there in the Malloy. Hell of a cop. Unbelievable instincts. Could find a clue in a clean room. He broke in that semi-weird Jap lieutenant when he was a rookie. You know, the guy with the stick over in homicide. Nice guy, Mike Hamilton. You'd like him."

"What's that gotta do with this shit tonight?"

"Ah, nothin'. Just doing this one in his neighborhood, that's all. He quit before you transferred up from L.A. Went to work for the *Chronicle*."

"Another step down, huh?"

"I see him now and then around town. Covers city hall now." Joseph shook his head and laughed. "Nutty sense of humor on duty. Always kept me laughing. Got him a whatcha call it, Pulitzer Prize, a couple years back. Shit, it was nationwide. Even on TV news night after night. Did one of those investigative things. Helped break a drug syndicate in the East Bay. Maybe, so far, the biggest in the state."

"Yeah…yeah, I remember that. They ran the story in L.A. too. So, how come a hot shot Pulitzer prize reporter lives in the Malloy?"

They had come up out of the Filmore and the fringe of the lower Haight-Ashbury District, and were just passing the elderly brick buildings of Franklin Hospital. In the distance, they saw the lights of Malloy Street. "Don't know. He moved in there after the fire. He…."

"Fire? What fire? You're rambling, Willy."

"Mike's house. Nice little place out in the avenues. Thirty-fifth, thirty-sixth…out my way. Word was, about six months after the bust, the operators who survived with their skivvies still on burned him out. Set his house on fire one night when he was out."

"So? He got lucky." Morgan picked some tobacco off his lip and rubbed it from his finger onto the shotgun barrel where it hung on a second, then fell into the darkness under his feet.

"Not quite. His wife and two kids were sound asleep inside."

Morgan inhaled sharply and held it for a second, then let it out with a rush of air, like a large animal sensing danger. "Hey, do me a favor, Willy? Don't tell me no more of those. Already, I got enough."

Crossing Market, the tires were jostled by trolley tracks. They saw the car parked a block away up the street. "There's Two," Morgan observed. "Now what?"

Joseph sped by the entrance to Moe's Saloon. "We circle the block a few times until Morrison and Three are in place. Then we move in."

Chapter Four

There was a split second of disbelief on the man's weathered face, but it vanished. Perhaps the boy knew something he didn't. The villager hurried out of the courtyard and down the mountain's treacherous path. Wo Chin turned to the cook. "I will prepare the hall to receive our guests. You make the tea. Bring sweet pickles for the children too."

More than two hours later, the villagers arrived carrying what little they could, as if believing that even the climb to the empty monastery was futile. They had no weapons and no experience in fighting. They were lost, soon to meet the fate of their friends and relatives from the village below.

A mist falling like quiet rain had begun as Mike stood on the concrete island waiting for his trolley. When it came, he went to the rear past an elderly, exhausted looking Mexican woman in a blue bandana. He also passed a drunk, snoring and smelling like sweat and feces, who looked like the side of his face had either scraped a brick building or the street. In the rear, a couple lights were out, and that's where Mike sat by the window as they moved in the outward current of Friday night traffic.

He touched the jacks ball in his pocket, turning its scared surface with his thumb and first finger. He had seen the flame's glow illuminated against the mist of a night sky just like tonight: the sporadic rhythm of fire truck and police lights so intense that they seemed to form a blinking red wall before his vision. He parked up the block as close as he could get, and broke into a dead run, knowing it was his house and fighting an even deeper knowledge as he ran. He broke through the police tape, passing the firemen who were shouting at him. But that was all. The windows had shattered on both sides of the front door, consumed by the flame leaping across the red brick entry and porch. He could only stand, watching the last of Julie's flowers in the redwood planter disintegrated by the door.

Mike had wanted to throw himself into the fire, because he knew. It took three firemen and two cops to subdue him. They were gone. They. Were. Gone. He said the words silently over and over as he sat with his in-laws in the dark living room of their home and watched the fire burning in the hearth until it went out and dawn crossed their hook rug and hardwood floor. Gone. Never to return. And he could have prevented it.

It didn't have to happen. He knew he could have prevented it as he walked at dawn through the still charred and smoking remains of the house and found only the jacks ball in what used to be the hallway by the door to Caddy's room. He had wanted to name her Caddy because Faulkner's line always clung to him, "Caddy smelled like leaves."

They had been taken away. Whatever "they" had become. The church told him the place was called "heaven" unless you had sinned. But Julie, Caddy and Mike Jr. had never sinned, and what did the church know? What had it ever known? Julie took the kids to mass regularly. Had he gone, would a voice have told him, during the intervals of trying to join in prayer with them, to leave the East Bay drug story alone?

"Ex-cop wins Pulitzer Prize." The champagne had flowed in the newsroom that day along with the hugs, handshakes and back slaps. The special dinner with Julie at Ernie's. How bright the future looked. The book offer.

The trolley pulled up at the island at Market and Van Ness and the driver shouted back at the drunk who didn't move. The driver cursed and came down the aisle, shaking the man until he wobbled upright and hung onto the chrome pole by the rear exit. The drunk managed to get on the step that triggered the door, and the traffic noise flooded the silence along with the driver's cold voice asking the drunk if he could make it across the broad street. The man nodded, stepped down to the bottom step and lurched onto the cement island as the double doors swished closed. He hung on to a light pole there as the trolley bell rang and it pulled away.

After the fire, Mike had lived in a clean hotel downtown in a room with a combo fridge, oven and two top burners. But he was only there to sleep, whenever that happened. From the first day, his friend, Jon Lee Koshima, had been there for him. Weeks passed. He'd worked fourteen-hour days at the *Chronicle* when there was less than eight hours of work to do. Jon Lee's mom, Anna, had him over for more dinners than he could count and offered him her upstairs flat that was soon to be vacant out on 24th Street in the Malloy District. Mike couldn't go back, let alone rebuild the house, so he'd moved into Anna's on the same day the settlement money had arrived. What good was the money, a sick joke?

More weeks passed, but nothing changed. How could he pray or ask for miracles when there could be none to grant him? At the point when he began thinking about taking his own life, he'd finally decided to take the help offered by Jon Lee's brother, Naga. He was an orthopedic surgeon who'd decided for reasons he never explained to add the discipline of psychiatry to his practice, and would see Mike as part of his residency. Even in his state of mind, Mike couldn't help smiling about being in the hands of an orthopedic-would-be-psychiatrist who charged him nothing, saying he had enough interns on his couch to cover the costs.

But after months of weekly sessions, there had been no explaining away the grief, and Mike had quit. It was then that Jon Lee made a strange suggestion. Jon Lee was still teaching at the Kiwan, and he asked Mike to come there to talk with Yee Chin.

After Jon Lee departed, he sat with Yee Chin on the deck of the inner courtyard by the Koi pond. The rock garden had sand swept like the sea amidst a series of rocks that looked, the longer Mike sat there, like the islands of some distant and mystical archipelago.

After a long silence, Yee Chin and said only, "We think that death is real. But it's not." Somehow that simple yet incomprehensible statement unleashed all the guilt and grief, and Mike poured it out as if he couldn't stop himself. He'd cried openly in front of a man who was almost a stranger, and when he was finished, Yee Chin only touched his arm firmly and said, "You can stay as long as you wish. Help me cook and do the chores."

Mike never left the Kiwan until the day he departed weeks later. No writing, no work, no contact with the outside world except for the street noise of Chinatown that rose in the early morning and at sunset. He had done what he'd never done. There was the hall, practice room and temple to sweep twice daily, and he'd wash each on hands and knees after lunch. He'd read nothing, and at first when the chores had run out and he paced the hall or sat watching the students in the afternoon and evening, he didn't think he could take it another minute. But then he'd retreat to the Koi pond and sit in the sound of the small waterfall that fed it. There, something he never understood returned him to a sense of peace, as if writing, reading and other responsibilities beyond the walls had no meaning in that moment.

At the end of the fourth week, Jon Lee had shown him how to sweep the sand by the Koi pond and that also became Mike's job. He found his work an embarrassment next to Jon Lee's smooth strokes, but somehow it didn't matter to Yee Chin if it was perfect or not. But whatever he was doing, the grief remained by his side like three ghosts and a world without meaning beyond them.

He and Yee Chin hardly spoke, and Jon Lee was unusually quiet as well. Yet by the end of the sixth week, something he still did not comprehend began to happen. Slowly the grief and guilt began to become like a friend you have so much in common with that it's sometimes hard to be together. And still, you want to be. But somehow, he vaguely understood that it would remain with him always, just like Julie, Caddy and Mike Jr.

The trolley stopped at the Twin Peaks tunnel, and he crossed Market and started the climb up Castro. Pausing, he stared at all the lights that rose abruptly from the business section into the two-, three- and four-story houses and apartment buildings, some dating back over seventy-five years. As he passed the bank, the Polish Deli and the Laundromat, he could see the misty letters of Moe's bar. The right half of the neon "M" flickered sporadically, with long periods of going dark that turned the sign into "Noe's."

After eight and a half weeks away from everything he'd ever known, Mike went back into the world again. All Yee Chin had said as they stood in the cool morning serenity of the entry was, "Now, live as best you can, Mike, but always bring yourself back to the moment."

He still had no idea what had happened to him in the Kiwan, but he was slowly piecing together a life in Anna's flat. He'd built some redwood planters on the roof to grow some organic vegetables and flowers. He'd kept his furnishings almost as sparse as the Kiwan had been.

There was no understanding it, any of it. They were gone and the wheel kept turning. It was just Friday nights when the grief lost its compassion and covered him. He passed the custom leather shop that the hippie couple on his block owned. They'd drifted over, like many artisans, from the Haight-Ashbury over the years to set up small counter culture businesses. Billy and Ellen. Characters. Good people. Lived just across from Anna like the gay couple who owned the pet shop across the street from Moe's. Also, good people. No cleaner pet store in the city, he'd bet on that. Mike looked up once more from the sidewalk to the sign. He had to smile as he went through one of the red double doors into the laughter and hum of the Friday night crowd.

The place was jumping. Billy, Ellen and a group of the new arts scene merchants in the neighborhood had two tables pulled together amid beers, nuts and chips while Paul and Jack, the pet store owners, sat quietly but happily apart taking in the scene. There were also the Greeks, who lived next door to him in two tight circles, one men and the other women, as pipe smoke rose like a funnel from the former. So many of the faces were familiar, but he was surprised to see Mr. and Mrs. Dobkovnic, the retired Russian couple who Anna had told him moved from Detroit where the old man once owned a small tannery for shoes and hand bags that his son now ran.

Tonight, they had their daughter-in-law and son and even their little five-year-old granddaughter, Natasha, with them—all squeezed together in the far corner. The old lady kept giving a stern look to her husband who seemed to have made one too many toasts.

"Hey, man," Billy shouted as Mike passed on his way to the far end of the bar, "Sit, man, we're talking Dickie Nixxxon."

Mike shook his head. "Maybe after I christen my pew," his thumb jerked towards the end of the bar, "I'll stop over. Keep Dickie warm!"

Billy burst into laughter. "You got it!"

He made his way slowly to the end of the bar. All the round and multi-scarred wooden tables were filled, and there were even people standing by and uncomfortably sitting on the old brick of the empty and now non-functional fireplace on the back wall. Moe was running up and down the bar like a crazy man, dodging his two assistants and trying to keep up with the orders for the waitresses. As always, he wore his standard black tee shirt which revealed the numbers on his forearm like a soldier would wear his medals.

Moe had been in the camps from 41' to 44' and somehow survived. Relatives in America contacted him in '45 and he'd come, just a boy of fifteen, to his new home. He was a super patriot and cynic combined, with a wit that always bordered on the bizarre, sometimes even losing him customers. One example of this was the tattoo he'd had done just above the concentration camp numbers on his forearm. It read "Hi, I'm Moe. Have a nice day!"

"Same o' same o,' Mike?" Mike nodded and squeezed onto the last barstool that Moe always reserved for him Fridays, no matter when he wandered in. Moe raced off to pour the glass of house red wine. He held it high, weaving between his assistants, and brought it down in a smooth arch in front of Mike. "So, how goes the week?'

"Down and dirty. Time to till the vegetable garden."

"Oh, thanks for the cucumbers and lettuce, by the way. Brings back memories of my step old man's garden. Real taste, not the crap we get down at the market. Kids today probably think milk comes from a dairy case." He smiled.

"I didn't know that." Mike looked dumbfounded.

Moe chuckled. "Back to work but had to do my weekly checkup on you. See any cuties this week?" "Yes, as a matter of fact. But all too young."

"Crap on that. You're what, forty-two? Then I'd say twenty-two is within range." Mike toasted him and laughed. "Try it, you'll like it."

"Who knows?"

"The wife wants to set you up with her niece but I said, no...o...o. That's up to you."

"Tell her thanks." Moe motioned, and hurried back up the bar.

Maybe, maybe, Mike thought as he took in the scene and another sip. The light was intense from the three formal chandeliers that Moe had salvaged from an estate sale's reject pile. Mike had yet to figure why, but Moe spared no expense having them cleaned and polished once a month. Unfortunately, they had no dimmer switch.

He sat quietly. A woman about thirty-five was sitting mid-bar and they smiled and mouthed "hi" to each other. She was wearing black pants and a white turtle neck which couldn't disguise her dancer's body. Her light red hair was combed out tonight, and it matched a complexion full of freckles that always made him imagine that she'd just stepped out of some crazy alpine meadow. He motioned and she came down the bar with her lime water.

"Evening." He got off the stool and let her sit down.

"You too." There were no two ways to cut it. Teri may have been past her prime as a dancer but she was still very beautiful. "How come you never call me?"

He smiled. "I'm sorry."

"So, I'll be the feminist. I'm putting the finishing touches on next week's performance tomorrow morning but I'll be finished by one. How about lunch?"

"Okay."

"Don't be so enthusiastic!"

Mike looked down and little Natasha was standing by his side. She had a little napkin with a drawing which she was offering to Teri who bent down, kissed her check and took it. "Thank you, Natasha."

Teri rented a little cottage behind the Dobkovnic's
house. She and Mike both waived at the family as the
little girl retreated into her grandfather's lap.

"I'm sorry."

"Damn, don't be sorry either."

"Deal"

"Good. Come to the rear door of the opera
house. I'll leave your name."

"Thanks…."

"What was that?"

Mike had heard it too. It was as if someone had
been hit hard in the stomach. Suddenly there was
shouting by the front entrance and six men were forcing
their way through the crowd. He recognized an old
acquaintance from his days on the force, Willy Joseph.
They weren't shoving people aside—but close to it—as
they came through the crowd. Four stopped at Billy's
table, and the others in front of Paul and Jack.

One put his hand on Billy's shoulder, and Billy
shoved it away and stood up. Joseph and his partner had
gotten a terrified Paul and Jack up, and were escorting
them through the crowd amidst cat calls and cries of
outrage. "You fucking SID bastards!" The cop next to
Billy shoved the end of a night stick in his gut and he
fell back into the chair.

"What's the charge, you apes? Give me a
charge!" Billy was shouting as one put the night stick to
his throat from behind and the other three managed to

force his arms back into a pair of cuffs. It was then that Ellen threw herself at the three of them, pulling hair and clawing until they managed to slam her against the table and into cuffs.

"What the hell?" Moe had come down the bar and stood in front of Mike and Teri. "Mike, they got a right to do this in my bar?"

"It's crazy. It's got to be a mistake, Moe."

"Well, somebody better be payin' for it. You know any of them?"

Mike pointed at Joseph who had almost reached the door with Paul and Jack. "Yeah. He was in homicide with me. He's been over at SID since."

"Can you do anything, Mike?"

"Joseph is an honest cop. This is crazy. Let me go out and see."

There was a kind of low keyed bedlam in the street as customers poured out of the bar under a starless, grey-black sky. Four unmarked cars sat in the lane across the street. There was one SID in the rear car whose face was obscured. He didn't get out as Joseph and his partner helped Paul and Jack into the rear seat of their car.

Billy was another matter. Four of them had all they could do to force Ellen and then Billy into the second car. When the door closed, Billy's shouts of indignation could still be heard and then his boots were banging on the window until it cracked. Mike was sure he saw one of them stuff a small white plastic bag into Billy's vest pocket. Mike ignored one of them who motioned him back to the sidewalk and flashed his *Chronicle* badge. Willy Joseph was just starting his engine when Mike reached him. "Willy?"

"Mike, what the hell?"

"That's what I was wondering. I can vouch for Paul and Jack."

"Mike, you know me, so listen. Back off quick. Please. I don't know anything. The captain…" He pointed with his thumb over his shoulder to indicate the rear car. A beer glass hit the rear door, and Mike flinched. "…captain said pick 'em up. I pick 'em up. I gotta go. Drugs or something."

"Come on, Willy, and what's all this SID stuff this past month? You guys are terrorizing the neighborhood, for chrissake."

"I'm not deaf, dumb and blind, Mike. Shit. I gotta go. We never had this conversation, please." He revved the engine.

Mike backed away and re-crossed the street as the cars pulled away amidst more shouts and the sound of broken glass against metal. Teri and Moe stood on the sidewalk in the crowd. "Better get everyone back inside, Moe, unless we want more of the same."

Moe shouted to the crowd. "Okay, everybody, inside for a free round." They cheered and began to file in. "You comin', Mike?"

Mike shook his head. "Enough for one night."

"Mind if I walk up with you?" Teri asked. He extended his arm and she wrapped her fingers around it.

"Mike?"

"Yes, Moe."

"Have you got a clue?"

"No. The cop I know wouldn't say and he looked scared himself. Okay. I'll look around. Maybe my friend Jon Lee knows something."

"All this SID crap, Mike. These are innocent people, for God's sake. I gotta run and call Harve Felstein, he's the best attorney we got around here. It's starting to get real nasty, you know?

"Yes."

Moe folded into the crowd and disappeared inside as the two of them climbed the hill to 24th.

"Would you like to come up for a nightcap?" Mike offered as they reached their street and turned right onto the last row of old Victorians below Mt. Noe.

They stopped by his steps. "Yes. But I don't think you're ready for me to come up yet. And I'm starting at seven in the morning." She reached up and kissed his cheek.

"Night. See you for lunch."

"Night."

Chapter Five

When they were settled on the mats of the temple floor, the cook and Wo Chin served them tea. No one spoke. Only the children smiled, happy with the sweets. The others stared in contempt, resignation and fear at the two who served. Then Wo Chin approached the elders. 'You must wait here with the rest.'

'For what,' they asked, 'your brothers?'

'I will go down the mountain.'

The laughter of the elders pushed against the silence like a beast ready to devour them. 'Why boy? To try and save your own skin?' Then he turned and was gone.

Maque, handpicked by Esse's son Abyase to live and work in the Holy City, had been found to be a traitor attempting to sell the little he knew to an American in what he thought was a Cairo CIA safe house. He was wrong. The American agent was left headless and handless in the entry hall, and Maque was returned to the Holy City.

"For this he must die, Rasheed. There can be no question." Abyase spoke in a low, calm voice, but after a friendship that had lasted since childhood, Rasheed knew that it was the way his friend talked when he was on the verge of violence in word or deed. Abyase had found Rasheed in the streets of Mecca. He was nearly starved and covered with sores. But Abyase brought him home where he was fed, clothed, healed and taken in like a son by Esse. No one, perhaps even Abyase, worshiped Esse as did Rasheed, and his devotion might soon lead to his marriage to Esse's only daughter, Dama.

The concave walls of the corridor carried them in the sterile source less light down a slight incline that ended at an opening across which was hung a thick white and yellow Oriental rug pulled partially to one side and held by a brass ring. Beyond lay an enormous room whose floor was partially sand covered with Oriental rugs of various sizes and shapes facing an altar on a slightly raised platform. It resembled an ancient dolman with a thick, flat slab of white, grey and black marble, twenty feet long by ten wide by two feet thick. The support rocks at either end were each ten feet in circumference and appeared to be machine tooled while the marble slab was rough and uneven as if it had been pulled from the wall of a quarry and made smooth only on the upper surface which held a single gold, finely carved pitcher. The ceiling here had the cast of blue sky through light mist. There was a similar entrance on the opposite wall from where Abyase and Rasheed stood and there was a rock formation next to the altar from

74

which water cascaded downward from the high ceiling into a pool that never overflowed.

A dozen men in the oatmeal robes sat on pillows on the rugs with Esse at their center and facing the altar. The sound of someone moaning seemed to echo down the far passage until it took form as a man with a dense black beard into which dried blood from a gash on his temple had settled. The robe he wore was filthy and his arms were bound back tightly. Two enormous men carrying swords that were long and slightly curved, looking more Samurai than Arabic, shoved him to the center of the room and he stumbled and fell to his knees.

His eyes wildly searched the faces of the twelve on the pillows until he saw Esse and shouted, "Mercy, Holy One, mercy!"

"I will give you mercy, traitor!" Abyase came from beneath the hanging rug, drawing his own sword as he came. He brought it up quickly, slicing downward to precisely catch the top of Maque's left ear who let out a scream of pain.

Esse had risen and come forward. "Abyase!"

Abyase bowed but gave no ground. "He is my traitor, father. My mistake."

"Is our way without any mercy, my son?"

"Father, he has betrayed everything we hold sacred!"

75

Esse hesitated, turning to look at his council of advisors. "Our way for a traitor is the desert with a day's ration of water and food."

"I want him cut enough that he bleeds slowly, hanging in the main gardens by the fountain for three days and nights. As we approach our opening into the world, I want anyone with Maque's ideas of treason to think twice when looking upon him!"

A look of shock seemed to ripple across the faces on the sand as Maque tried desperately to crawl towards Esse as he called out, "Please, please, Holy One, please. Mercy!"

Abyase hit Maque's head with the glancing blow of his sword. "Silence, animal!"

Maque moaned and shook with the pain but didn't move further.

"This has never been our way, Abyase."

"You have given me the choice and I have shown you my way. I await your decision and, as always, will abide by it, but there are times…."

Esse's raised hand stopped his son's voice. He looked down at Maque. "Maque, Maque," he said with deep compassion. Then he walked directly to the altar and picked up the pitcher, carrying it to the waterfall under which he held it. As he walked back to the center of the altar, Maque screamed for mercy once more to be met again with Abyase's sword.

But he would not be silenced. "Holy one, master!"

Esse lifted the pitcher and walked along next to the marble, letting the water fall upon it and trickle into the sand from one end to the other until the vessel was empty. Maque screamed again as they hauled him out the way through which he came, his pleadings echoing in the passage until the room was silent. Esse bowed to the council and to Abyase and Rasheed who returned it. The council rose and followed him out under the white and yellow Oriental rug.

As he made his way to the laboratories in the deepest center of his world, he prayed that he would come to understand why his only blood son clung to the old ways despite everything he had been taught by him and the Master Tutor, Burta, who had supervised both Abyase's and Dama's education, even accompanying them during their years away at university in England to assure that they would live and continue to think in ways of peace not violence. Perhaps Panjali would have some thoughts to share.

Esse had bid the council farewell and now walked alone, except for a single tall and hooded figure behind him, onto a moving sidewalk that began a slight decline. He touched its support railing once with his palm and the sidewalk moved faster, rounding curves and corners, ever downward until, in the far distance, the passage slowly widened and the sidewalk slowed and ended in what appeared to be a solid granite floor. The white walls and ceiling were also granite, as if he was coming directly into the hard rock of the earth itself. Directly in front of him the wall was as smooth and hard as black marble, and as he opened his palm towards it, it parted in the middle. The granite beneath his feet began to move and he was transported into a green mist as the wall instantly closed again.

Sounds like a computer or radar tracking began but these seemed distant, like that of small animals in the dense growth beyond a forest's path. They stopped just as quickly as they'd begun. The mist vanished. The floor moved again and a second black wall of ivory parted as he was carried into the main research laboratories.

Here the dream he had envisioned almost since childhood had come true. Here the opening of his vision into the world would begin. From here, peace would come to the planet for the first time.

For such a vision, the main room was very small, no bigger than ten by ten feet. All the walls, except the one from which he had entered, ceiling and floor appeared to be the same hard black marble substance. The difference was that these must have been transparent because through them came an ongoing series of varied colored lights flickering on and off intermittently, while in other areas many series of numbers and letters never left the wall but constantly

78

changed to form new groupings. Directly in front of Esse at the center of the room stood the chief scientist, Panjali, with both hands on a raised desktop that seemed to mimic the walls. As his fingers moved across the board, pressing here and there, the patterns on the walls altered while he spoke in Arabic into a head set.

"Tuning the piano as always, my old friend," Esse smiled.

Panjali held both his hands above his head, palms pressed together in greeting, but didn't turn around for several minutes as his hands went back to the black board of lights, letters and numbers. His hands moved even more rapidly, like a classical pianist reaching the dramatic climax of a concerto. Abruptly, he stopped, threw down the headset onto the desktop and wheeled around with an enormous smile that seemed to radiate from his deep-set brown eyes.

Compared to the oatmeal robes, he was oddly dressed in a *Los Angeles Lakers* purple and gold tee shirt and basketball shorts to match that reached well below his knees, with a pair of wraparound sandals covering his bare feet. His appearance was made more comical by the fact that he was only 5'6" tall. "Oh, what a day, what a night, master!" He exclaimed in his clipped Hindu-British accent and bowed. His dark brown cheeks had a three-day growth of beard, and the tee shirt looked as if he'd spilled something on it. "When did I sleep last, who knows? But, ah! What results!" Esse extended his arms and Panjali touched them to his cheeks.

"I have been watching you, closer than you think, and neither of us has the strength of youth to endure this anymore. Yes, my old friend, you have not slept in three days and that is why I have come, to find out when you plan to do so." They both laughed and Esse reached out and grasped Panjali's arms with affection. "Well, what is your answer?"

Panjali stepped back and raised his arms as if to embrace the entire laboratory. "I can finally sleep. Oh, master, oh old friend, we are connected and cross-connected and every single test, done three times each, has been a complete success!"

"You mean...?"

"Yes," he interrupted. "Absolutely. We now control both the American and Russian satellites, which gives us pinpoint accuracy. The American one will beam your vision into the auditorium at the Palace of the Legion of Honor when you give your 'surprise lecture'," He chuckled, "while the Russians, those devils, will secure the essence of our power on the exact coordinates just below Mt. Noe.

"Yes, yes. Your Designate 8's construction project should begin immediately. I have outdone my own prediction by almost six weeks. I still am in disbelief, but the proof is here." He gestured at the walls and the control desktop. "The seven western states, western Canada and all of Mexico are now open to our options."

Esse took both of the smaller man's hands in his, and they looked at each other in silence until tears began to form in their eyes and they hugged. "Panjali, my friend, you are the greatest genius this planet has known. May God be praised for sending you to me."

Panjali wiped his eyes and spoke with reverence. "I serve only your vision. It is truly the way for the world."

"Thank you. Without your vision, loyalty to our vision and dedication, this would still be what we first spoke of in Mecca thirty years ago, when we were deciding between guns and science, war and peace."

"And lucky for us you decided against being an illegal arms dealer and I turned down General Motors!" They laughed again almost in unison, but Esse was suddenly silent. "Your thoughts are heavy, master. Can I help?"

They left the lab and stood in the entry's green mist. Esse shook his head sadly. "Abyase."

"He's young."

"I've tried since his mother's death and Dama's birth to instill in him a peaceful nature. But to no avail."

"You can't blame yourself, master. You've given him the best tutors, exposed him to world travel, been both mother and father for both of them, all the while building this holy city beneath the Sahara. You

81

have let him see what the world could begin to be tomorrow if it could shed its fears, its petty egos, and its desecration of God."

"But I have failed. You've certainly heard what he will do with the traitor Maque?"

"Yes. We are both saddened by that. But, perhaps, we both need a bit more faith in what you have given him. As I say, youth. This is his first real decision. From it, can't he learn?"

Esse touched Panjali's shoulder. "I would hope."

Panjali raised his hand, and the wall to the left opened. "I want to make a brief go around in the other laboratories before I sleep. Give Abyase a little more credit. Just a little more." Esse nodded and Panjali walked into the mist and the wall closed.

At the top of the decline, Esse walked from the conveyor down a wider hall to his left. The tall hooded figure had reappeared a few feet behind him. He was greeted by those who passed with palms together and a slight bow which he always returned with a smile. A few minutes later, the passage he was in curved gently to the right. Two men, also robed and hooded stood to one side and bowed as the wall opened and he came into his own quarters.

It resembled an oasis. A few feet inside, the hard floor turned to sand and rose slightly to one side where there was a broad tent set next to a pond of clear, dark blue water with a dozen date palms in bloom not far back from the edge. He entered the tent, whose floor and walls were decorated with Oriental rugs. Other than some silk pillows and a couple of ornately hand carved leather trunks and a low table, there was no furniture.

Dama rose from one of the pillows as her father approached and they embraced, kissing each other's cheek. They sat next to the entry where the palms and water were visible. "Well, my Dama, how do you like your part as the servant girl so far?"

"Don't you mean, 'servant woman,' father?" she teased.

"All right, all right. Your years in London now come back to haunt me." But he too smiled.

"Your Designate 8 is an odd duck."

"In what way?"

"He seems quite ill at ease, almost a bit frightened."

"And wouldn't you be, even with all your sophistication, if you were taken during the night across the Sahara to an underground place where you found a near exact replica of your home thousands of miles away?"

She pushed her long black hair away from her temples with both hands. Even though her high cheek bones were pronounced, there was still a gentle roundness to her face with its dark eyebrows and lashes accented by her contrasting hazel eyes that always reminded him of her mother's Indian origins. He smiled to himself. The great tutor Burta, and then school in London. An Arab-Indian raised with two Gods, Mohamed and Jesus.

"You're right, of course." She paused as if to think of how to go on. "I think he might try and seduce me if he could."

"Then we would be looking for another Designate 8 from the Sector 1, wouldn't we?" He smiled.

"Why don't you tell me your whole plan? All this talk of Sectors and Panjali down there in the nuclear lab. Even he puts me off."

"It's all harmless, my dear. All part of our peace plan."

"And how will Abyase fit into that? I'm told Maque is to be hung in the main convergence by the fountain. That is not our way of peace."

He patted her hand. "No, never."

She ran her hand across his left cheek and jaw. "The weight of the world is tiring you, father. You need a rest. Let's go to the Mediterranean."

"Once all is in place. Once you return from your mission to America. Then I will be able to rest."

"This American is so strange. All the power at his disposal in his own land, yet he carries himself without confidence."

"They are a weak people with little self-esteem. And does it matter so long as he wants what we want?"

"I guess not."

"Then let's treat him as the honored guest he is." They both rose and walked to the wall beyond the pond. "Just so long as he doesn't make advances."

Chapter Six

*As he descended, the last of the summer flowers
in reds, yellows and purples hung in crevices in large
moss-covered rock formations. Wo Chin hardly noticed
these, his own fear was so great. He could climb above,
hiding until the marauders had killed, burned and gone
away. He wanted to. Once he did step off the path, but
returned, continuing until he reached a clearing, a
place where the path opened to an overhang, flat like a
plateau, about ten feet wide by twenty-five long before
it narrowed again on the other side in the descent to the
village. There was nothing to cling to at the edge of this
place; on the one side was the mountain's smooth
surface and on the other, a drop of at least five
thousand feet into a canyon of razor-sharp granite
spires. Even with the mid-afternoon sun on the path, he
shook with a chill that reached outward from his bones
as he heard the bloody cries of men climbing the path.*

Mike found the usual junk mail in his box at the
top of the high, wide porch. He heard the Dobkovnic's
gate open, and saw Teri's silhouette pass through it to
her cottage. His lobby's hardwood floor creaked as he
stepped inside. The door to Anna's flat was just slightly

ajar, and the light from the crack and from the leaded glass panels stretched just to the edge of his feet. He started up the stairs and Anna stood, short and stocky in a violet, rose and blue muumuu, in the light. "Where you think you go and not say hello Friday night?"

Mike smiled and looked down at her. "I'm sorry."

"Apology accepted. Dinner ready. Jon Lee is here." She glanced over her shoulder, shook her head and frowned. "Drinking again," she said softly. Mike shook his head just as Jon Lee entered the door frame behind his mother. Though Mike figured he'd had plenty to drink, Jon Lee never moved with anything but his normal grace. "Hey, hey, reporter-cop. Drop down for some tempura. I'll pour you some sake and we can forget about Friday night."

"Thank you both, but I've got some leftover pizza that won't go another day. Throw together a salad. Just left a bad scene at Moe's."

"Que pasa?" Jon Lee asked.

"I don't know. SID pulled Paul and Jack and Billy and Ellen out in handcuffs. Willy Joseph was there. He looked scared and confused. They planted a bag in Billy's vest when they were wrestling him into the car. Somebody in the crowd must have seen it too. You have any idea what's going on lately with all these phony traffic tickets? Jack told me they've had health inspectors twice in the last three weeks."

"That pet store is cleaner than any restaurant in town."

"I know. You hear anything?

"Some scam about the mob trying to muscle in on the last of the hippie drug scene like they did in the Haight. Crazy stuff like that." He paused. "Bet that beautiful ballerina 'cross the street would make that salad better than you." Jon Lee's laughter was harsh, as if he'd told a bitter joke. He was always louder when he drank; that was the only indication. He didn't wait for an answer, but turned and went back inside. Anna closed the door, and came closer to the bottom of the stairs.

"Naga want him to go rehabilitation clinic up at hospital."

"Anna, you know Jon Lee's more disciplined than any clinic could ever make him."

She wiped her left eye with a finger and looked at the stairs. "He so depressed about his work. Even say he thinking about quitting."

"He could teach. He's practically got his Ph.D. thesis done. I knew when I had enough."

"But you not drinking."

"Anna," he touched her chubby hand which was resting on the banister, "I'll talk to him again. You know how much he's helped me."

She grasped his hand and shook it. "I'm sorry for both of you. Life impermanent, the Buddha say. But why so hard on us sometimes?"

"If your meditations give you the answer, please share it with me."

She smiled. "Thanks for talking to him." She turned back to her door and he continued his climb to the flat.

He stood motionless inside, leaning against the closed front door. Streams of yellow light from the lamppost across the street worked its way through the natural pine shutters he'd installed on the street front windows of the living room. The light first dispersed through the four hanging ferns he'd put by the windows above a double bookcase that ran the length of the wall under the windows on which healthier looking plants sat. Plants he'd had twenty years, even more, had died in the fire but he still had the green thumb. The hardwood floor, without even a single area rug, held the spiny shadows of the plants like the moon through a cedar grove would on a pathway traveled only at night by nocturnal forest creatures. Though he'd purchased an attractive canvas and wood couch, a long and generous coffee table with inlayed top, and three forest green director's chairs, the room remained like the forest path where no humans had come.

As his eyes drifted, he too saw just the motions of a life, not like the house with Julie and the kids or his parent's retirement place down in Big Sur. Those had and have the sense not only of living beings' present, but a welcome to others that was so obvious that a stranger would immediately exclaim, "This is such a warm, homey place."

He crossed the darkness and under the arch into the small kitchen with its single shuttered window and single fern. He took the pizza out with some salad fixings and a half bottle of white wine, and poured a glass. As he made the salad and let the pizza warm, he fought to keep Julie and the kids at bay. Memories were nothing but the jacks ball now.

He sat on a bar stool by the counter, and finished the salad before walking back into the living room with just the wine. Through the partially open shutters, he could look up beyond the Dobkovnic's where Mt. Noe grew steeper. The moon was in the last cedars. He'd never tell anyone that they, those wonderful trees, might have saved him.

Too corny for an ex-cop and a reporter, but many nights during the past two years he'd gone stealthily by Teri's small cottage and quietly made the climb to sit watching the lights of the city and their reflection on the far water, sometimes until dawn. There were stories, ancient and modern, about old trees having cared for people just in their presence or the touch of their sap. And there was really no reason to continue living. Half his life gone. All its meaning gone.

What was happening in the neighborhood? It couldn't be drugs. Whatever it was, the ongoing SID presence had created a tension where there had been none before, and that was saying a lot for an inner-city neighborhood where tensions should run higher given the ethnic mix of Blacks, Irish Catholics, Orientals and Mexicans. Even the beat cops were feeling the tension. He'd talked to a couple of old timers he'd known for years. Why did it have to come to the Malloy District? He'd had all the trouble he could handle. Why did this have to follow him too?

Mike put the dishes in the sink, then walked down the hall past his little office, the bathroom, and into a bedroom of ferns and plants, with a queen-size bed. He could lie and look out the two broad windows down across apartment and house back yards of junk, grass and clothes lines, and over the edge of Franklin Hospital's fortress shape on the distant hill with the hint of wharf and downtown lights beyond. An hour later he fell asleep in his clothes.

The red glow of his clock on the night table said 3:45 am. Whatever the sound that woke him was, it came dimly from the street in front, like a chime only more mushy like coins shaken in a tin cup. Lights from a dark car forced two men across the street to shield their eyes as they stood talking to two others whose

backs were to Mike. Then he recognized Paul and John.
One of the faceless figures was holding a set of keys,
and kept shaking it close to the two men's faces
followed by his flashlight washing over the rest of their
bodies.

The front door was already open and Anna
stood on the steps. "Who those guys with Johnny and
Paul?"

"My guess is probably yours too. SID"

He walked down the steps and she followed him
out into the street. A light went on upstairs in the
Dobkovnic's and two of the Greeks next door were on
their porch. The one with the keys wheeled around,
startled, and the other grasped his baton in its holster.

"Who the hell are you?"

"A neighbor. Those are my neighbors. You guys
SID? What the hell's going on?"

"You don't ask the questions, buddy."

Mike raised his wallet and spread it open so
they could see the plastic I.D. holders on each side, one
with his retired police badge and the other his
Chronicle press card. "Okay, buddies?"

"These just got released and we followed the
sweethearts home to make sure they got here okay."

"Looks like they did."

"Yeah. Let's go, Jack. Standard police business,
Hamilton, nothing more."

"You stay 'way from us," Anna called after them as they got into the dark car and backed down the block to Castro. A brick came out of nowhere, like a bat from the trees on Mt. Noe, and hit its hood, but the car sped up in reverse onto Castro, then disappeared down the hill.

Anna hugged both men. Their normally neat appearances were rumpled, and exhaustion had spread across their faces. But this had not extinguished their anger and humiliation.

Paul stared toward the corner. "Those filthy bastards! I'm sorry, Anna."

"They are, Paul. Why they stop you again in front of your own house?"

"It's 'bash a queer night,' Anna, hadn't you heard?" John said and kicked out at the air with his foot.

"Did Harve bail you out?"

"Yes, Mike. He's down there still working on Billy and Ellen. They said we were picked up on suspicion of …. Jesus….of soliciting," Paul said with a shrill disbelieving laugh. "Morons!"

"What?"

"Then, after almost seven hours in a cell with a pig smelling of booze and urine, they dropped the charge and let us go." Anna hugged them both again and Mike joined in. All the house lights on the street were off again.

John looked at their house. "Look at that place. It's beautiful. Two years we took to restore it. It's perfect. We run the cleanest pet shop in this damn town, and have been cited twice in the last three weeks for nothing, petty crap. We're model citizens, goddamn it!"

"What do you think is happening, Mike?" Paul asked. "You're in the know down at city hall. We feel like just taking the offer on our place. It's an absurd amount, just like Homer Thween. Enough for us to buy a beautiful cottage in Carmel and even a shop down there. We went around with a realtor last weekend. But all our friends are here, and half of them live within a five-block walk."

"I was talking earlier today to a woman I know who works in the mayor's office. She told me about Homer selling too. Something about a condo project they want to build and the developer, a jerk named Locke, needs your houses. Just out of curiosity, when did this all start for you?"

John stretched and rested his arm on Paul's shoulder. "God, I don't know. A while ago. We got stopped twice a few weeks ago, coming out of Moe's. Pure harassment."

"Any time around when the house offer came in?"

Paul and John looked at each other. "No, before that."

Anna clapped her hands together. "Okay, enough for now. You two try to sleep. You have work tomorrow, Saturday a busy day. Mike say he check around. He get Jon Lee to help him."

They hugged again and walked to their houses. It was 4:40 am, and Mike made a pot of coffee and took it upstairs to the roof. If there was no connection with the real estate offers that all but Thween had refused, what then? The sun was on the other side of Mt. Noe, but it had begun backlighting the trees.

Chapter Seven

At his side of the overhang, Wo Chin stood in near catatonia, hands leaning for support on a gigantic rock which must have weighed four or five tons and measured ten to twelve feet in circumference. What was he to do? His panicked thoughts boiled. Such a fool! He should have fled! But no time now. They would be on the other side of the overhang soon. They would be upon him.

His hand began to feel the cold stone pressed hard against it, and he set his cheek and forehead there beside the hand in a thin layer of moss. The soft coolness revived him a little, enough that he began to cry softly. He was going to die; there was no doubt in his young mind. A slow death they would make of him, painful, even if he tried some defense against their overwhelming numbers. When the monks returned, the monastery would be burned, drenched in blood and slaughter. What had forced him to come this far? Let the villagers meet their own fate. Why hadn't he hidden?

Designate 8 awoke abruptly from a horrifying dream in which he was being chased by several

individuals in oatmeal robes. He was running through
an unknown forest, and all he could see of them were
the robes and the moon glinting off their high-held
broad and curved scimitars. He was sweating as he sat
up too quickly, and the room spun as the dream was
replaced by his insecurity that somehow his
presentation wouldn't be enough, that the twenty
million he was getting wasn't being earned fully.

He was still concerned, even after Dama had
bought him his desired breakfast of hash browns,
sausage and eggs over easy, as he and Rasheed
traversed one corridor after another. Rasheed carried
the briefcase and he was just beginning to relax when
they came around a curve into an enormous public
gardens and fountain, complete with grass and trees and
a ceiling as blue and bright as an October sky in San
Francisco. What he saw as they passed through the
center of the gardens nearly made him vomit. Hanging
from a post was a terrarium in which a man was hung
by his feet. Its walls and ceiling were covered with
bubbles in various shades of red from the transpiration
of liquids from the body which looked as if it has been
slashed a hundred times with a blunt garden rake.
Rasheed's only comment, as Designate 8 staggered to
keep up with him, was, "Maque, a traitor."

He was still mildly hyperventilating when the
wall opened and he entered the private quarters. Esse
came from the tent and shook his hand. "My friend, are

97

you all right? You are pale. I can summon a physician."
He glanced sternly at Rasheed who meekly replied, "by
Abyase's orders" and bowed, backing into the corridor.
The wall closed and they were alone.

"No, no sir, I'll be okay."

"Come, sit here by the pond." Dama came from
the tent with a tray of fruit and cold glasses of water
and tea. "Please, try this tea. I know it will settle your
stomach quickly." He settled himself on a pillow next
to Designate 8. "My deepest apologies. That was my
son's doing, you must understand, not mine. He has not
learned the way to peace yet. I can only hope."

Designate 8 drank the cold tea, trying
desperately to block out the scene from the garden, and
almost immediately he began to relax and feel his
stomach settling. "That's like a miracle."

Esse nodded. "There are many here, my friend."

Designate 8 suddenly sat as erect as he could,
given that he seldom sat cross-legged on the floor,
which made his stomach protrude even more. He
snapped open the briefcase and rummaged through the
papers until he had them in a neat pile on the rug.

"I wish I had more progress on the real estate,
but so far we've only managed to purchase one of the
four houses. A retired plumber. I don't know why the
others hold on when you consider the offer. Heck, it's
easily double what those old houses are worth."

"An old neighborhood, it's understandable the ties to such false sentiments people have." Esse paused to drink some tea and eat a section of a tangerine. The silence began to make Designate 8 jumpy.

"Well, don't worry, they'll sell. We're taking steps to make it pretty uncomfortable for the other three. There's a couple of queers and some people left over from the sixties."

"You call them 'hippies'?" Esse chuckled.

"Yes, that's right. Our strategy is to work on them and then focus on the last ones, some retired Russians. I figure that by the time we convince the queers and the hippies, the Russians will fall in line quickly."

"I have received some very good news this day from our chief scientist. Certain connections and experiments have been completed early, so the need for construction is even more pressing."

Designate 8 began to worry that the twitch in his cheek would start up, but even through his nervousness he felt calm. It was something about Esse's serene manner.

"So, the sooner the better. Offer more money if needed. Americans always enjoy money, don't they?" Designate 8 nodded. "It is not critical that the entire project be complete, but certain internal aspects must be in place by next May, just a year and three days from now."

99

"That'll mean really rushing the plans through and getting permits."

"Yes. We must be ready for the United Nations fiftieth anniversary since it began in your city. Officially that was January 1st, but because of certain scheduling and other diplomatic conflicts, the date has been set for the week of May 21 through 27."

"That's right," Designate 8 interrupted. "Reservations are already underway at most of the big hotels. That's going to be something."

"Your Palace of the Legion of Honor?"

"Yes. I understand that the Vice President will be attending."

Esse's face changed and he smiled impishly. "And I will be a guest speaker."

"You will? I don't understand."

"I share that with you in complete confidentiality and trust."

"I won't breathe a word."

"I know that. And the how and why of it will be revealed to you in good time." He reached over and picked up a single piece of drafting paper by his side and unrolled it, placing two of the dishes on it to hold it open while he and Designate 8 held the other ends. "Only those in my deepest trust and yours will ever see these plans."

Designate 8 recognized the original plans he had seen for the Corfu Village project, but these contained an addition which looked like a tunnel going back directly from the underground parking into the hill side. It split into three different directions. Two were dead ends and the third appeared to be a small room. The index finger of Esse's free hand moved up the tunnel and stopped at the room. "This is the essence of why we build this project. We are not interested in real estate developments." He smiled. "In this tiny room deep in your Mt. Noe soon will rest the first step in our vision of world peace. That is why by next May it must be fully functional, even if the building is still under construction above it."

Esse rose and Designate 8 struggled to his feet. They walked slowly across the sand to the white wall. Esse held out his hand, and they shook for the first time. Designate 8 noticed that Esse's hand had only the thumb, index and middle finger. Esse unselfconsciously held up the hand. "My father worked for the British to build the trans-Sahara railroad. He was really a slave, not an employee. We were nomads forced into the white man's work. Though I was very small, all boys over seven had to work as well, and my fingers were cut off between pieces of track that were being laid."

Esse paused, his jaw seemed to tighten and Designate 8 almost shuddered from the anger he felt from the man. "They gave us no medical attention and my father held my hand in the cooking fires to stop the bleeding. They gave us no medical supplies. There were no doctors. Just the desert." He studied his hand for a moment and sighed as the tension subsided. His face was almost serene again when he looked up and sighed. "My mother died out there too. It was a harsh time for us all, but that was what formed me. That was when I knew I must devote my life to world peace, to healing the world."

The wall slid open and Rasheed was standing there. Esse took up Designate 8's pudgy hands and held them. "Now, move this project quickly so that the day of healing may come all the sooner."

He released him and Designate 8 found himself bowing slightly. He could feel the twitch begin again in his face. Had he done a good job? Esse seemed pleased. But the rage, the anger he had felt from the man? It seemed so out of character, given the mission they were on. He had no idea what time of day it was, but he badly needed a drink when he got back to his quarters.

Designate 8 had hardly left when Panjali and Abyase came from the opposite direction and joined him, Dama and Rasheed by the water. Panjali set down his briefcase with a grin, and snapped it open. Though looking like what business people carry, this one was unique. Inside was a blue screen on the fold-down side, with a series of lights and switches on either side and below, like a laptop computer, was a keyboard, also with switches on one side. It came on instantly. There were only three files titled "Neurology," "Bio," and "Stress Conversions."

"Here he is, the rotund little fellow." He pressed "Bio," and a series of medical charts whose information, mostly numerical, continued to fluctuate. Everyone bent forward to look at the screen. Panjali motioned to Dama. "Here, my dear, show us what you have learned, since it will be you and Rasheed who will now take my place with monitoring the little butterball."

He positioned the screen so that she could read it more easily. "What do you want to know?" she asked with confidence.

"Well, what is he doing right now."

She glanced at the screen, then made several keystrokes, each time pausing for a few seconds. "He is drinking his scotch, and rather early in the morning I'd say." She opened the "Stress Conversion" file. "What did you say to upset him, father?" Esse shook his head and Panjali moved closer to her.

"You can refine this."

She nodded, pushed her long black hair away from her face and typed something else. "You frightened him, father. He's reliving your conversation about your hand. He was unnerved by your anger."

Esse acknowledged. "Yes, even after all these years it rises and falls. Panjali, my basketball fan, you have made even more improvements. You are able to convert the neurology into images?"

Panjali laughed and grinned even wider. "And continuing to refine that, my master." He turned to Dama. "And?"

"He is very happy to be going home today."

"With our new tracking system inside him," Rasheed said, and even Abyase laughed. "It is truly amazing what one glass of American beer with a little extra added can do."

"It is untraceable, will not break down and will be with him to his dying day," Panjali commented as he continued to look at the blue screen. "Even the subtle impression of a nightmare will be converted so that we will understand even more about him. As soon as Dama and Rasheed have set up shop in San Francisco, they will be able to relay all this to our laboratories. I will have analysts and psychoanalysts on duty 'round the clock to assure that our Designate remains loyal and trustworthy."

"I still believe, father, and you, Panjali, that he should have our tracking be known to him to further assure his loyalty and trust."

"But why, Abyase? We don't want him to suspect because that would put him on his guard." Abyase acknowledged Dama's words.

"So, Rasheed, prepare to take him back to Mecca and prepare yourself. The chartered jet for you and Dama is standing by so that you will arrive long before he does. I would like to say goodbye to my daughter."

"Oh, master, forgive me, but one more item. I just learned what that construction in the Sierra Nevada Mountains east and north of San Francisco is. The Pentagon has been concealing funds for three years now to build a new missile assembly and launch base in a rural area called Kennedy Meadows." Always one to love the dramatic, he paused and looked at everyone. "These are nuclear weapons that will be capable of striking targets from Canada to New York to Central America…and China! A bonus delivered into our hands." Everyone clapped and bowed to him. Then they rose and moved to the open wall. Just as he was exiting, Panjali turned and said with a giggle, "And don't forget your briefcase, Dama."

They both smiled as the wall closed, and Esse looked at his daughter. He was about to speak but she raised her hand. "I know, I know, father. But there surely must come a time that you can release me and not worry. After all, I spent all those years in England."

"But with Burta, your tutor, and our people to attend you and Abyase."

"Father." She leaned forward and kissed both his cheeks and let go of his arms.

"All right. I can't be that different than other fathers whose daughters go half way around the world

105

into a strange and hedonistic land devoid of both God and faith."

"Rasheed will protect me with his life as will the protectors you send with us. And this Huntington Hotel on Nob Hill is both beautiful, safe and the perfect spot from which to monitor Designate 8's daily activities." She closed the briefcase and picked it up.

He walked her to the wall. "I will be anxiously awaiting your twice daily communications." She kissed his cheek again, and as she stepped into the corridor he said, "I lost your mother at your birth."

"You will not lose me"

Chapter Eight

The boy dropped his bamboo staff and fell to his knees as if letting go of life itself and all the responsibilities he could not meet and would never have the chance to, letting go of his burning desire to be a Master of the 12th Circle of Zahu. Letting go of everything he had ever held as worthy and sacred, he awaited the barbarian with dry eyes.

It was in that moment of utter release that the boy experienced what none of his fellow monks ever had before; he felt for an instant that his body was filled with light and the world around him had become more radiantly alive than he'd ever experienced it. It was as subtle as a dawn breeze, here and gone, but the grace of that moment filled him with such heat that he was perspiring through his robe.

Mike felt the first warmth as the new sun began to filter through the cypress and pine, spreading down through the shadows of the Malloy District. He'd come straight to the deck with a coffee after the incident earlier, and was weeding the six beds of vegetables in their raised redwood containers that he'd constructed last summer when he moved in with Anna. Now at the end of June, a few tiny leaves in the red and green leaf lettuce bins had begun to sprout, along with the first radishes and a hint of some carrots. After the Pulitzer, he was hoping to move south and into the valley out toward Yosemite. The acreage was cheap and it was close enough to the city to commute a couple times a week to write his thrice weekly political column.

The roof door scraped open, and Anna came out onto the asphalt roofing with a sack in her teeth and two mugs of steaming coffee. "I go right past your door, but don't knock." She said in a muffled voice. "Knew you be up here." She set the coffee down on a weathered picnic table, and put the bag down too. "I make biscuits for breakfast with ham and egg, but Paul and Jack say they go right to work. Here." She handed him a hot biscuit. "Eat this, then come down in a few minutes for breakfast." They picked up the mugs and toasted.

"I will talk to Jon Lee, Anna."

"I know, Mike, you will." She walked over and looked down through the yards three floors below and then up toward Franklin Hospital and beyond toward the outer bay. She didn't cry but he sensed that she wanted to. He put his arm around her. "I don't understand nothing. Ever since father died."

"Anna, he was twenty-two when he came to work with me as a rookie. It's been almost twelve years. And four in homicide. There's lots of people that don't last two in that department."

"Maybe police work is waste of his life. I never like."

"I know. I've encouraged him a dozen times to try and get on at city college in the criminal justice department. He's got the master's degree, is working on the Ph.D., and all the experience. He could eventually teach there and keep helping Yee Chin at the Kiwan. I'm sure when Chin dies that Jon Lee will take over the teaching."

"Yeah, but that teacher part may be just dreaming. Like you, all the time even when you were policeman, always dreaming. Justice. Good for everybody. No more killing or bad guys. I listen to you two talk lots of times. Even Julie...." Her voice trailed off.

"She always thought I was a dreamer too."

Anna stood up straight and looked up to him. "Cannot change that, Mike. I always so sorry. You and Jon Lee looking for justice in a world always fighting. Greeks next door fighting with each other, police fighting with gay people, Oriental, Black, Mexican. Then war. One after the other. I'm glad you guys dreamers. I'm sure Julie was too. But hard world for dreamers. So many ignorant people, stupid, mean. I wish I could go back to Japan sometimes since Yoka-san die. But that a dream too." She took his cup. "Okay, five minutes and you come down for eggs."

After a breakfast much lighter than Anna planned for him to eat, Mike went back up to the deck and worked until almost eleven. Anna had brought up the Dobkovnic's granddaughter, Natasha, and he'd given her a place to dig and a small spade while he continued to work and talk to Anna. There seemed no reason for the SID acts in the neighborhood, but to him there had to be a connection between what happened early this morning and getting everybody across the street to sell. If someone had the power to get the SID involved, mob stories aside, he'd worked too long doing investigative reporting not to know something strange and serious was going on.

He'd just come out of the shower and was toweling off when the phone rang. It was a classmate from Berkeley who had, for reasons known only to him, always managed to keep in touch. In fact, he was one of the first to offer help after the fire. Andre was calling from his car phone, and in the background Mike could hear the roar of the DB4 Aston-Martin, Andre's pride and joy which he'd modified to go much faster than it was ever intended to go. "Dear boy, I've been thinking of nothing but Sears' pancakes surrounded by their home-made maple syrup and those perfect sausages. Are you ready for a breakfast-lunch?"

"When, O' noble large one?"

"You needn't rub it in. I'm passing Candlestick Park now so it should be less than twenty minutes."

"I'll be downstairs." He hung up, called Teri to cancel their lunch, and began dressing. Andre Duman was just a year younger than Mike, but to Mike the man had lived many lifetimes. He'd quit MIT after his first year in the physics doctoral program because, in his words, "They had nothing to teach me." It was then that he set up a lab on his estate within walking distance of Stanford. His assistants had been just students he'd taken up a conversation with on benches, young people he sensed were not willing to live their lives in a world of illusion, but wanted to get a handle on reality.

He was feared and hated and denied by many of the science and academic community, but in that lab, employing a hand full of mavericks like himself, he'd contributed to the hard and medical sciences. Like all geniuses who live on the margin, he was feared and denied because he always challenged the rigid militancy of the status quo and was hated because his immense fortune gave him complete independence from the world of mortal man.

Mike never understood anything Andre would try to explain to him when they'd tour the labs on the occasional weekends that Mike would spend there swimming in his Olympic pool, heated with a system of Andre's invention, and wander the gardens. What he did know was that, maverick or not, Andre had close ties with most of the important minds in science and, unbelievably, with the international intelligence

111

community, loving stealth most next to science. He'd been an accomplished pilot since his teens, and now spirited about the country and globe on any whim in his Lear 36. Andre had flatly refused to fly a fighter jet in Vietnam and, through family influence, was assigned to fly B52 supply runs during the war.

He could hear the engine roar from three blocks away and then the flash of British Racing Green coming around the curve to park in front of Mike on the wrong side of the street. As usual, Andre was in his standard uniform of open white shirt with paisley ascot and blue blazer, baggy brown wool slacks and white Tretorn tennis shoes without socks. "I hate driving into this damn town. No speed and the 'great unwashed' trying to coordinate their brain and gas pedal to something around twenty-five miles per hour down these wonderful streets that could be used for Grand Prix practice if they weren't in one's way. Jump in old boy."

For an extra ten dollars, they parked in the St. Francis Hotel garage, and walked the few blocks past Union Square and up the hill on Powell between Bush and Pine where Sears Restaurant was located. They'd been eating there for twenty plus years since college, when Andre would insist Mike drive over with him at least twice a week. Andre never spent a day in the city without stopping there, and the owners and most of the help called him 'Herr Andre' because of his girth,

boyishly round and healthy face and a long mane of
blond hair that seemed to scatter everywhere around his
forehead, ears and down over his shoulders. They
ordered the usual, and drank fresh orange juice and
coffee while they waited.

One of Andre's most endearing qualities was his
concern for others. Never had Mike heard Andre
discuss himself and his work without being asked.
"Well?" He stirred a little cream in.

"I'm doing okay. Even met a nice lady."
Andre's thick eyebrows raised and lowered. "She isn't
pushy. Patient. I don't know. I'm also getting bored at
the paper."

"You could have done that column and be
working on that book. My God, looking a gift horse in
the mouth if I've ever seen it, considering the advance
they offered you."

Mike disregarded this. "I mean bored in general.
Ten years. I drive out to the avenues once in a while.
Brand new house there. Real nice. They keep it just like
we did. Sometimes I think I'd like to follow through
with my plan and move over toward Yosemite."

Andre stuck his napkin into his shirt in
anticipation of the pancakes and sausage. "Not working
out up there at Jon Lee's mom's?"

"It's deeper than that. Can't articulate it yet."

The food arrived and Andre focused on pouring syrup and spreading butter. "I don't see how you can eat like that."

"My cholesterol was 310 a year ago. As a side project, I studied the science."

"And solved that problem, right."

"Right as rain, Michael. Nothing for the FDA to admire, but it's all organic and my count is now 190."

"What can't you do?"

"I haven't reached that yet. I'll let you know." He took up some pancake and sausage on his fork and chewed it slowly. "My God, wonderful. We are an emotionally stunted country, but when we do pancakes and sausage right, we do them right. So, tell me, what is all this SID chatter you told me about in the car? The Gestapo is restless?"

"The pieces seem to fall together like this. The developer, Locke, wants the four houses across from Anna's so he can build something called Corfu Village, a three-tiered condo project, each with broad balconies, the old Aegean thing. One guy has sold, and the others don't want to go. Somehow this is tied up with Shelia Vernin, the vice mayor—maybe she's pushing it through for Locke, I don't know. This morning about 3 am, some SIDs were harassing the gay couple across the street, and the leather smith and his lady didn't get in until around 5:30. Both were picked up at Moe's by SID last night. I saw them plant a bag on Billy and the gays were charged with solicitation. Billy's charge is still pending but Paul's and Jack's was dropped."

Andre wiped his mouth but didn't speak immediately, his gaze roving across the group of impatient tourists milling around by the door waiting for a table. "What does the inscrutable Oriental who carries bamboo staff have to say about all this?"

"Jon Lee seems in transition right now. I think he's sick of all the crap in homicide."

"The revolving door of justice?"

"Right. Kind of lost, bitter…and drinking way too much. He hasn't been able to return to the Kiwan yet so there's that, too. That's really his life."

"Well, he's certainly handsome enough to find a love interest if he chose to. The same diversion I'd prescribe for you."

Mike laughed. "For Jon Lee, the women have always come and gone with barely a caress. And, no, he's not gay. I'd know that after working with him for years. I'm going to try and look him up after we finish. He's kind of like you are in the scientific community, Andre, only he's the odd man out at the SFPD. I still know a lot of the guys. Maybe between us…." Andre nodded. "What's up with you, lad? It's been at least a month."

Andre finished the last of the pancakes and his face became just slightly serious. "I'm afraid I don't know anyone intelligent in the SFPD except a former member and a strange but likeable Oriental, so I'm not much help." He leaned forward. "But I have something to share that's troubling me. You can't solve it but I'd just like to air it with the friend who counseled me after my first failed attempt at sex as a freshman." Mike smiled. But Andre was serious.

"A very strange event has just occurred that appears to have been undetected by anyone but me." He glanced around to see if anyone might be listening as if by chance a KGB double agent disguised as a forty-pound overweight, tanless male or female tourist might be listening.

"You're being serious now, Andre? I don't always know, since over the years I've mistaken serious for kidding more than once."

"Serious. Somebody is playing piggyback with two major satellites, one Russian and one ours." Mike shook his head. "Somebody is using these for their own tracking purposes. I've modified the cutting-edge technology for my own purposes, which means out beyond the cutting-edge, and there is no indication either Russia or us realizes somebody's up there with us."

"What does that mean?"

Andre drank the rest of his orange juice and smacked his lips. "Ah, good." He twirled his glass as he set it down. "How should I know? What I do know is that the signal is coming from somewhere out in the

Sahara, north and east of Mecca and landing right here
in this city…where it vanishes just like it does in the
desert. I can't locate it. It just disintegrates before
landfall, probably because they haven't chosen to
activate yet. I've made a bunch of discreet calls to the
kids who should know—haven't defined it for them
though—and they don't."

"Then what could it mean?"

"It means there's somebody out there with
better technology than me. And that pisses me off! But
in a less ego-driven vein, the world's superpower,
paranoid as we are about security breaches, would be
busting a gasket to find out."

"Sure, if they knew."

Andre smiled. "I'll let'em twist in the wind a
while until I nail something down. Are you ready?" He
paid the check. Andre had to go to his tailor for a fitting
downtown, but before he drove off he promised to ask a
few people he knew at the federal level locally if they
knew anything about the SID-Malloy connection.

Mike picked up the Hyde Street cable car at
Pine and hung on the outside with a Saturday load of
tourists going to Fisherman's Wharf. It was just past
one, and he had a hunch. At the last stop, he walked by
the Buena Vista Café and crossed over to the Aquatic
Park gazebo and small park that surrounded the cable
car turntable, down through the grassy knoll past the
South End Rowing Club and along the concrete apron

117

that curved around in front of the Maritime Museum. Traversing the bocce ball courts where the language changed abruptly from English to Italian, he headed out for the fishing pier that jutted out into the little bay towards Alcatraz Island and the Golden Gate Bridge.

There was half a dozen or so fishing, and at the furthest point he saw Jon Lee. The bamboo staff which never left him was tucked into his belt behind his back. There was a small fishing tackle box near his feet, and the camel's hair jacket was neatly laid on the waist-high concrete wall. The line on the rod drifted in the current, but Jon Lee seemed to have little interest in it as he gazed back at the wharf and some of the fishing boats, who still birthed there, returning with the day's catch. Though he didn't move, Mike knew that his presence had been known to Jon Lee since the cable car stopped.

He walked up and put his elbows on the concrete railing and looked where Jon Lee was staring. "A good day."

Jon Lee remained unmoving. "For what?"

"Banana fish?"

Jon Lee had to smile and turned to look at Mike. "Always the witty literary type."

"Figured I'd find you out here."

"My old man started dragging my mom, Naga and me out here when I was still in a sling on her side. We'd make a day out of it. She'd bring lunch and he'd hold me right here with the rod in both of our hands.

The recreation spot for immigrants," he motioned toward the bocce ball courts, "away from the city and always looking in from outside."

"You did pretty well; two degrees and a Ph.D. in the works."

"Only sort of in the works." He took up the line on the reel but it was slack. "Did the world do pretty well by us, Mike?"

"It's always given us a few choices: me, the citizen, you, the nationalized citizen. I didn't have to follow the leads on the South Bay drug scene. As a former cop, and since it was inching in over onto this side of the bay, I guess I had no choice. I just don't know what the choices are right now. Julie and the kids aren't coming back."

"Nobody leaves, Mike. Nobody dies."

"I wish I could see it the way you and the Buddha do. I can't."

"I'm sorry, that's not what you needed to hear."

"Well, I came out to see you for two reasons, not that one. How are you, and what do you think of this SID situation in the Malloy?"

Jon Lee reeled in the line, tied it off and leaned the rod on the concrete. He took the bamboo staff from his belt and began tapping it lightly on the railing. "Like you, I'm surviving. Going through the motions, wondering about choices too, wondering where the richness of things has gone. The richness is what I miss

119

most. There was real purpose at the Kiwan. Teaching the kids, just being with Yee Chin. When he put me out last year…," he shook his head and ran both hands through his hair. "I don't know. It always got me through the numbness of homicide work." He was silent.

"And it wasn't really even the work, the investigations."

"It's when all that's over, and you take it home."

"Yeah, but you know that, you've been there. You broke me into it."

"They go free on some legal technicality."

"Or plea bargain themselves down to a sentence that seldom matches the crime. We had one a couple of months ago. Guy takes a kitchen knife to his wife in front of their five-year-old, and Murder One is dropped on an evidence issue. Is there anything just?"

"They aren't physically killing themselves in the corporate world, but look at all the bodies—jobless and desperate people—that are lying around after a downsize or merger. Or the FDA lets them market a drug that a year later turns out a killer, not a healer."

Jon Lee picked up the fishing tackle box and set it on the railing. "This is the perfect spot for us. This wharf. Outside looking in." He smiled. "Come on, I gotta go practice down on Ocean Beach. I may be becoming a drunk, but I'm still practicing."

"Maybe that's the route for you right now towards that 13th Circle of Mastery." Jon Lee nodded.

"Okay, Mike. I'll drop down to Chinatown this afternoon, and see if I can find *the Noodle man*. I don't want Mama worrying herself over it."

"Thanks, I'll poke around downtown next week, give old Bear Danielly a call. He can't be happy with his precinct going to hell."

Jon Lee shrugged half-heartedly. "Maybe we'll find something interesting." Mike started to speak but Jon Lee raised his bamboo staff. "If it's another South Bay, I won't let you get involved."

"Maybe that's what I need. Revenge."

"Attack. Revenge. Yin and Yang. Energy's neutral. It can go either way."

Chapter Nine

Abruptly, what he must do crystallized before him. Picking up his staff, he stumbled behind the rock, wedging it beneath the stone. With legs planted firmly on the sloping ground, his thin shoulders against the rock, he began to push, to heave upward, never thinking about the absurdity of his action. His body must have strained against the enormous mass for several minutes without letup, and he could feel a numbing exhaustion sweep into every fiber of every muscle. Yet he continued, as if that strain and fatigue were not with him, until, with an echoing explosion, the tons of granite lurched and rolled across the monastery path, blocking it. The boy fell and lay breathing hard. His muscles ached so that he could barely sit up. He stretched his arms and legs until, finally, he could stand without falling. Perhaps the rock would give the villagers a few minutes more of precious life.

On the next Tuesday, Jon Lee dropped by his mother's home for lunch. He'd been to Chinatown twice, but had not stopped to see the *Noodle man* yet. It was a perfect fall day in early spring with a cloudless sky and a sun just warm enough to be comfortable in all day. He parked his unmarked blue sedan in front of the Dobkovnic's, and waved to the old man who was contentedly sitting in a rocker sipping a beer in front of the double garage doors near the front stairs where he could move in and out of the sun, depending on his mood. Twice now, police in unmarked cars had stopped and threatened to ticket him for drinking in public, which he'd been doing without incident for the past three years.

He opened his mother's door quietly and moved in silence as he'd been trained across the living room and down the hardwood floor of the hallway past the dining room on the left, and the bath and two bedrooms on the right. The last door on his left was the kitchen, and she was just setting down steaming bowls of noodles and vegetables when he snuck up behind her and quietly said, "boo."

"What! Why do you always do that? Someday, boom, I have a heart attack on this floor. What will you think of yourself then?"

He bent down and kissed her forehead. "It'll never happen."

"How do you know? I'm getting old and stiff."

"You're only sixty."

"Your father."

"Age doesn't count with cancer." He sat where he always sat, at one end of the kitchen table which was positioned in a three-window alcove offering a slightly lower version of the view from the roof.

Anna carried over a small crystal pitcher of soy sauce, and sat in the chair directly facing the view. Whenever her son, Naga, joined them, he sat at the other end. "Why, Naga not coming? He didn't call."

"He had an emergency surgery this morning and he's still doing it. I called the hospital. Besides, you know he always calls when he can." She frowned. "So, anything else exciting happening around here?" He poured soy sauce on his noodles.

Mr. Dobkovnic always had a beer before lunch. Even when it rained, he'd stand inside his garage until his wife Jeanetta called him in. The front door at the top of the stairs was open, and he could hear Natasha laughing, helping her mother and his wife in the kitchen. The family had come from Detroit, their original home, for his birthday, and his son and daughter-in-law were going camping in Big Sur for a few days, leaving the little girl with he and Jeanetta.

A faded metallic blue '85 Mustang with a patch of rust on its top turned slowly off Castro onto 24th. It was moving slowly, almost cruising, and the engine rumbled as if the muffler was about to break. There were two men inside wearing baseball caps and sunglasses, and Mr. Dobkovnic quickly shielded his beer under his light cotton jacket. They glanced at him in passing just as Natasha called from the porch to her grandfather.

His mother could sometimes give him a sense of calm like Yee Chin, and Jon Lee could feel it today. She had even offered him a beer, which he knew she didn't want to, but he took a Pepsi instead. "I wish you find a girl."

"I'm always looking."

"Why can't you find one?"

"Momma, come on."

"You find out anything about this SID? Two days ago, the Greek ladies were washing a rug on the sidewalk like always, and a couple of those guys started giving them a hard time, said they'd get ticket next time they do it." She shook her head. "I'm worried."

He reached over and caressed her shoulder.

The Mustang had turned around and began to accelerate, the muffler blathering louder and louder the quicker it came. Natasha came down the steps. She had on some new Mary Janes they'd bought for her yesterday along with a blue dress with white whales on it. "Go slow, my little girl. You don't want to fall."

She waved and smiled at him. "See, I'm fine." She was too short to hold the railing, so she clung to the banister legs as she descended.

Suddenly, the noise of the muffler seemed to overwhelm the street as the car came full tilt down the block. Mr. Dobkovnic put his beer down to help Natasha on the last few steps.

"That's gunfire," Jon Lee shouted and was down the hall and into the street before the car made the corner. Mr. Dobkovnic was cradling Natasha as her parents and grandmother came screaming down the stairs.

Jon Lee jumped into his car, rolled into a U-turn and had his red light on the roof and siren going before he skidded into the curve and onto Castro. The Mustang was weaving wildly through noon traffic, careening off parked and moving cars as it went. When it reached Market, he was only two car lengths off its tail. "24 Koshima in pursuit of a faded red Mustang, license Alfa, One, William, Niner, Seven, Five, Larry. Heading north on Market just past Castro. A 451 at 2724 24th. Ambulance!"

At the broad Van Ness intersection, the Mustang nearly took out the side of a trolley as it hit the curve on 11th on two wheels with Jon Lee right with it. At

Howard, the driver was going too fast for the turn and hit the trolley island, its rear end momentarily suspended until he managed to right the Mustang as it raced pass 10th, then 9th, 8th and 7th where, halfway down the block it made a sharp almost blind turn into an alley. Somehow, it was open except for the Mustang grazing a dumpster. It shot across Folsom into another alley and then across Harrison into another.

Jon Lee was tracking their route on his radio, and when the Mustang tried to cross Bryant, there was a black and white halfway blocking the alley to Brannan. The driver smashed into its front fender which whirled it out of his path, and almost hit Jon Lee who grazed it before plunging into the alley heading for Brannan. At Brannan, the Mustang went sharp left and put it to the floor.

They were entering the fringe of the warehouse district so traffic was lighter, but Jon Lee had to follow the other car's lead, weaving through trucks and people. Just before they reached 3rd, the Mustang went up over the sidewalk, knocking over a flower stand and momentarily obscuring Jon Lee's windshield, causing him to swerve wildly as they shot down another alley to Townsend.

At Townsend, they went hard left and then immediately hard right on 3rd, aiming straight into railroad tracks and open ground. A train with a load of container platform cars off a freighter was creeping slowing towards their path. The driver seemed to panic, veering first right then left until he lost control of the car and accelerated directly into the side of the train's second engine, but didn't bounce off. The car caught fire instantly and was being pulled along by the train. The driver managed to jump free and limped around the back of the train, firing back over his shoulder at Jon Lee crossing the open space and tracks. A battery of black and whites formed a wall behind Jon Lee's car as the driver disappeared. Jon Lee drove his staff into a place where the still moving car's door had collapsed. He couldn't stop his motion, but something in him stopped and with a single jerk the door fell open and the gunman's upper body fell with it. The lower half of his body was in flames and creeping upward as Jon Lee, in a single motion, pulled him free and cradled him in his arms, the flames catching the camel's hair jacket as he ran, carrying the man away from the train. They hadn't gone thirty yards when the car's gas tank ignited, sending off an explosion of sparks, metal and fire into the air.

He set the man down gently, and using his coat managed to put out the flames. There was no mistaking the smell of burning flesh. Jon Lee rummaged through the man's pockets, but he had no identification or wallet. The man opened his eyes. The eyes were empty. He was in shock. "Who put this out?" Jon Lee asked urgently. "Your buddy is gone. You're all alone now. Tell me, goddamn it."

The distant sound of an ambulance was coming closer. The man jerked with the pain. "You're going down alone. If you make it. Who put this out?"

"burr...bu...bah...winman.... bur...bird." Then he passed out.

A hand on his shoulder caused him to release the passenger, and he stood up. The medics moved in. "Save this one."

They glanced up at him. One with a shaved head looked up at Jon Lee. "Why, so you guys can work him over?"

"He just shot a five-year-old girl," he glanced at the man's badge, "Albert Wilson." Wilson looked back to the victim and Jon Lee walked towards his car, splattered with dead and dying cut flowers, and the sea of black and whites behind it. The right arm and shoulder of his coat was burnt, but it hadn't reached the skin and his charcoal slacks had a large hole in one knee. He held the bamboo staff with both hands as Captain Morrison came running from the line of police and fire vehicles.

"How'd you get into this, Koshima?"

"Having lunch with my mother."

Morrison glanced around, motioning to a dozen SID who hurried past them toward the accident scene.

"Terrible. The child is being taken to UC Medical Center."

"Why are your people ripping through the Malloy?" Morrison brushed off the question and started to go around him but Jon Lee moved with him, pressing the staff into the center of his chest and causing Morrison to jump back.

"Watch it, Koshima. You've always been on the thin edge, and striking a superior officer could just do the job."

"I'm sorry." He dropped the staff to his side.

"Look, Jon Lee. I don't like any of this any more than you, but the chief tells me to jump, I have to jump. All I know is what I'm told, though the mob angle hasn't turned up anything yet."

"What about my mom's neighbors, the hippie and the two gay guys?"

"All charges dropped."

"Your man stuffed a bag in Billy Richardson's vest. A friend of mine saw it."

Morrison started to move forward again. "That's bullshit and if I were you I wouldn't be throwing around accusations like that unless you've got more than hearsay." Morrison passed him and Jon Lee turned to watch him.

Then Morrison hesitated, stopped and turned back. "I know it's your mother's neighborhood, but you don't know what you're getting into and neither do I. If it comes from the chief, then it's bigger than either of us can handle. So, don't do any freelancing, understand, and don't encourage Hamilton—you saw what happened to him." Morrison turned back abruptly, and jogged toward the train.

Charles Locke paced back and forth on his broad, sweeping flagstone patio. On the table under the umbrella was the phone and his partially eaten lunch. The long, curled, white telephone cord to the mouthpiece kept whipping back and forth as he paced. Ever since the shooting the day before, he'd been trying to pacify Thween and Shelia. He was especially tired of Thween's incessant calling. "Thween, shut up for a moment and listen!" The man sounded hysterical. "Calm down, damn it, calm yourself and listen to me. I told you half a dozen times this was a crazy idea. I…I know the...your boss said we needed to speed the sales up, but I told you a dozen times there were a hundred ways to do that, none of which, you moron, involved bringing in a couple of gangsters I provided to throw a few rounds into the Russian's garage! All right, listen…listen…things happen. You fucked up badly! We move forward from here. If the child dies, you can't bring her back. Do you understand that? They've got one of the men and he's close to death from burns over

131

70% of his body. He's in and out of a coma. The other
one will be handled. Right now, you just mind your
own business. You've got enough explaining to this so-
-called boss about why you made this stupid decision. I
won't be calling you for a few days and you, damn it,
do not call me. Understood? Good? Now have a shot of
bourbon, regain your composure. Try to do some
packing to keep your mind off it. No, no, the police
won't question you again. They were just looking for
witnesses. Goodbye."

Locke slammed the phone into its cradle, and
took a sip from a glass of white wine by the lunch. He
walked to the edge of the patio, rubbed his eyes and
looked down at his yacht bobbing gently. "My
Windhover," he said softly as if acknowledging the
sleek blue and white vessel that he'd sailed around the
world on twice.

How could he have been such a fool himself to
let this idiotic plumber talk him into this hair-brained
plan? But what else could he do? He wasn't privy to the
so-called *boss*, so there was no way he could have
challenged the decision. Had the payoff not been ten
million for doing nothing but what he did, develop
property, he would never have done business this way.
The phone rang again.

"Yes."

"Charles!"

"Don't say my name again. Where are you?"

"In the mayor's reception area. Don't worry, his secretary is at lunch and he's on the phone."

"Go to your office and shut the door. Then call me back."

He took another bit of the roast beef sandwich but he barely noticed the taste. The phone rang again. "All right. You've closed your door?"

"Don't worry, my assistant is out too. God, Charles, we're in a panic down here. The mayor is going through the roof. I've never seen him so upset. The press is thirty deep down in the lobby, and he's scheduled to talk to them in a half hour. Please, tell me this doesn't have anything to do with the Corfu Village project, please. I mean, the Russian family didn't want to sell. Oh, my God!"

"Shelia, you have just two things to focus on and one of them isn't some horrible accident out in the Malloy District. First, the mayor, the Planning Commission and the Architectural Board of Review has okayed Corfu Village contingent upon my purchasing the other three properties. That's not going to change. Developers don't shoot into peoples' homes to get them to sell, do they? No. Absurd. Everyone knows this will be a real upgrade for the neighborhood and increase taxes and property values. That's why they approved it. And, everyone knows that if the dear folks won't sell within a year then I've wasted a lot of money and time. But they will sell, because I want that project, am

willing to offer even more, and I almost always get
what I want. Second, repeat after me…Mayor Shelia
Vernin."

"But…."

"Say it.

"Mayor Shelia Vernin."

"Done. We know he'll back you because he's
lost the edge since his wife went up to that sanitarium
in Napa Valley. And the rest is up to me."

"But…. I, how do I handle….?"

"Repeat after me," he interrupted her,
"Governor Shelia Vernin." She said it. "Six short
years, my dear. Those are your focal points. Now go get
him ready for the press conference. People are killed
every week in this town. I'm sure McGrady will see
this as a tragic accident, and that's how you want the
mayor to portray it, correct? Good. Now go do it and
I'll make some calls. Call if you need me."

"Thank you, Charles. It's just so unnerving."

"Accidents happen, Shelia. This changes
nothing. Pure coincidence."

"I can handle it, Charles. I've handled worse in
this office."

"Good. Now it's just a waiting game until those
three houses are mine."

Finally, he sat down to finish his lunch. He'd
talked to them all, including McGrady who had been
just as hysterical as Thween. Locke had reminded him

about the long view, the vineyard outside of St. Helena
that would be his in less than a year, and that accidents
were beyond either of their control. It had nothing to do
with the project, he had lied. McGrady vowed to find
the one that got away, and would be able to question the
one in the hospital if he came out of the coma.

It rang again before he could touch the Caesar
salad.

"Yes?"

"It's Robert, Mr. Locke." Robert was head of
what Charles Locke liked to call his "personal security
force" that always made sure that political and union
palms were properly greased for each major project and
assured that no interruptions in construction ever
occurred. They were the backbone of his reputation.
Subs knew that they either did it right and on time, or
their chances of making a further living in the Bay
Area, were slim to none.

"And?"

"We set up a meeting with him at the Oakland
dock warehouse for eight tomorrow morning."

"Good."

"I think we should have put somebody on that
Tenderloin hotel where they were staying. I'm sorry."

"Don't be, Bob. He may have moved on us, but
he won't be flying back to New York until he gets his
money."

"What about the guy up at UC. They got SID guarding him."

"He's close to dead. In a coma."

"Yeah, but...?"

"If he comes out, we'll deal with it."

"We've got some contacts there besides our administration link. Barney's kid's an orderly who wants to come to work for you. He's a good kid. An Army sniper in Vietnam, two tours and wanted to do three. Tight mouth. He just got married, and looking to do better than a two-bedroom apartment the rest of his life."

"Tell him to keep an ear open."

"Are you coming over after we pay this guy off and take him on his freedom ride?"

"Yes. I'll be on the boat, over around nine to take our friend for his last voyage. We can wrap this up by tomorrow night."

The line went dead just as the front door bell rang. He smiled with the thought of spending the rest of the afternoon with two of his grandchildren fishing off the dock, but as he walked in to greet them and his daughter, he couldn't shake off the one in the hospital. The one who'd escaped had handled the details. But what would the dying one say if he ever came out of the coma?

Chapter Ten

There was no time to reflect on what he'd just done, because at that moment a man nearly seven feet tall and wearing a bloodstained cloak of bear skin and eagle feathers stepped into the far side of the overhang. The warlord stopped, as did the horde behind him. Bracelets of gold, necklaces and rings of silver sparkled on each of them. The front four carried stakes upon which were rammed the ghastly blue-white heads of a man, a woman and two children. Wo Chin's eyes met those of the warlord.

As if seasonal morning weather hadn't come together until late afternoon, a gossamer fog floated in loose strands, interweaving with the declining sunlight over 24th. Mike, Anna and Jon Lee crossed the street. There was a navy-blue limousine across the driveway and two motorcycle police stood talking to the driver by the front fender as people climbed the wooden steps. Sue Obern was on the porch smoking, and Mike walked over to her as Anna and Jon Lee went into the front hall and across under the archway, hung now with fake ivy, into the dining room. Natasha's small open coffin was on the dining room table, and everywhere there were flowers.

Sue glanced at him and took a drag on her cigarette. "Unbelievable." He nodded and put his arm around her. "The mayor's really taking it hard. You know, a child."

Mike looked into the dining room, and to its right into the parlor. "Where's Shelia?"

"I came in her place. She was even worse off than the mayor. He knows lots of people out here. This was a big voting block for him too. He actually started to cry when he saw the little girl. Have you heard anything? I thought Jon Lee might…"

"He may have run them down, but we're all in the dark. I better go in." They hugged.

Mayor Hennessey's rotund figure in his standard dark blue suit was in the living room, leaning forward and engaged in conversation with Jeanetta who sat on the window seat with her son and daughter-in-law. The father seemed half in shock. He stared straight ahead without speaking while the mother dabbed at her eyes, listening to the mayor's quiet voice. Mike didn't know where to go. He couldn't go into the dining room.

Then he felt his arm being taken as Teri stood on tiptoe and kissed his cheek. "Open casket?" She nodded. The mayor made his good-byes, acknowledging Mike as he walked to the dining room, paused over the coffin, genuflected, and disappeared under the garlands of ivy.

"He was actually crying before you came in," Teri said.

"He's a politician, but a good soul. He really does love this city. Walk with me, will you?" She took his hand and they crossed the parlor to extend condolences to the family. Jeanetta got up and released her daughter-in-law's hand to kiss them both. "I don't know what to say, Jeanetta."

"You have suffered too, Mr. Hamilton. My son and daughter-in-law also know of your tragedy."

"You know, if I can do anything, I'm just across the street."

"Thank you, but with your friend Teri's help," she squeezed Teri's hand, "we will get on."

"Where's your husband?"

"In bed. Like my son, he just stares and says nothing." She looked around the room. "I guess the mayor is gone. I never expected him here."

"He grew up in the Malloy District, Mrs. Dobkovnic."

She shook her head and looked into the dining room. "We bury her here. We sell tannery and my son and daughter-in-law move out, live with us for a while. I hope they try again for a baby."

Suddenly, Natasha's mother lunged off the window seat and rushed to her daughters' coffin, trying to hold it, touching the little girl's surreal pink cheeks. "Natasha, Natasha," she sobbed uncontrollably until that seemed to awaken her husband and he hurried to her side with Mrs. Dobkovnic, the two of them pulling her as gently as possible back to the window seat as she resisted their efforts. They got her settled and gave her a pill, and Mike couldn't take it anymore.

"I gotta get out of here," he whispered to Teri, and they went immediately through the dining room and back out onto the front porch and down the steps. Sue was gone. Teri was already late for a rehearsal at the ballet, and she reluctantly left Mike who crossed over and stood next to Jon Lee's black '52 Porsche *tub*. Anna and Jon Lee joined him.

"That was a surprise," Jon Lee said.

"Yeah, but a kind gesture by the mayor. It didn't feel like politics."

"Maybe I've always misjudged him." Jon Lee took out his handkerchief and wiped a smudge off his passenger side rear view mirror. Anna said she would make them tea, and went back inside. "I'll go find the *Noodle man* now. Something this hot. He has to know." He got into the car and fired up the engine.

"What time is it?"

"Going on four-thirty."

"If he hasn't changed, Jake'll be up at the *Thigh and ?*, by eight or nine for his lunch break. He owes me." Jon Lee put it in gear. "Hey, no heroics, huh? If you get anything call me." Jon Lee gave him a thumbs up and slowly pulled away from the curb.

At about 8:30, Mike wedged his VW van into a parking space at the top of Green where it dead ends in Telegraph Hill just above Grant. He had come there by habit, because when he and Julie were first married they lived in a tiny one-bedroom in the last building on the block. Walking down Grant to Broadway, he looked into the windows of the restaurant, bakery and coffee shop they'd frequented so often. Though it had been several years, he recognized people who still sat at the same tables, the baker's daughter, older now, behind the counter, and another crowd of younger people probably looking for the same magic that he and Julie had found. The evening traffic was already heavy on Broadway where he turned left and headed down hill to the middle of the block. The signs in the windows may have changed along with the naked bodies and faces, but nothing had really changed.

The *Thigh and ?*—a pathetic play on words—had been owned by the same Chinese family since the early sixties, and miraculously kept transforming itself to fit the changing times. The new name was their attempt to combine sex with a fifties look and Country and Western music. It had long been the watering hole for SID personnel, and Jake was probably its best customer. They had once worked a case that overlapped with both homicide and the SID, and Mike had managed to get Jake out of a bad situation: drunk on duty.

Booths covered with plastic cowhide ran around the mirrored walls with tables holding a candle in a wine bottle on checkered red and white tablecloths. Red metal chairs and tables filled in the large open area in between the booths and the thirty-stool bar with its platform/stage dead center. Mike stood just inside the red-draped lobby where, even this early, two bouncers stood, dressed like cowboys.

The usual red, yellow and purple lights alternately twirled across the ceiling, floor and walls creating the feeling that it was a merry-go-round. Two dancers in G-strings gyrated slowly to the soulful moan of a cowboy who'd been done wrong. One was a cocoa-skinned black girl about six feet tall. Her thick black hair had been straightened but stuck out in all directions as if she'd hung onto too many exposed electrical wires. She had the tall, lean look of an athlete glistening with oil and sweat, and breasts that were way out of proportion to her thin body. Her makeup was probably supposed to make her look Egyptian.

The other girl was in total contrast: short, rosy-white skinned with white-blonde hair to her waist and the round body of a Rueben's painting, complete with thick fire engine red lips. They both looked bored or were saving the moves, grimaces and come-hither glances for later in the evening.

He spotted Jake in his usual spot at the far end of the bar. There was a girl no more than eighteen with ratty, short blonde hair and owl eyes surrounded by bad mascara sitting next to him. The cigarette she inhaled probably wasn't what it appeared to be. Jake was staring into the bar mirrors. He looked bored too.

"Mind if I saddle up for a few minutes." Mike squeezed his shoulder.

"Mike, the man. Good to see you." Jake motioned to the girl, and she drifted away with the sweet smell.

"Kind of young for an old guy." They watched her meander toward a booth.

"Any port in a storm." Jake was only half smiling. "Don't tell me you came down here 'cause you want to soak up the ambience. Hey, Tom, Jack on the rocks for my friend."

"Thanks." The bartender pushed the drink over to Mike. "I wish that was true, Jake. It's about the little girl out in the Malloy where I live."

"I'd heard you moved over there. I guess the pain must still be pretty bad."

"Comes and goes. How about you and Kerri?" He rubbed two days of grey-black stubble on his cheek, and took a large swallow from his vodka. "She got remarried about six months ago. Some old flame from school that went for the big bucks, attorney, and I guess he scored since they're living in St. Francis Woods.

143

Nah. No more tries at marriage for me. What about you?"

"Probably the same, I don't know."

"So, what can I do for you?"

"Explain what's going on in the Malloy. Why the phony parking tickets, pressing the gays, running the Health Department through my neighbors' pet store when it's the cleanest in the city. All that stuff. And now the child."

"You don't seriously think we'd…?"

"No."

Jake lit a cigarette and Mike sipped his whiskey. "You saved my ass, Mike, but what's said here tonight dies here. Have I got your word on that?"

"You know that, but, please, no talk of the mob and drugs. I know everything there is to know about that."

He snorted and let some smoke drift towards the dancers whose faces and rhythms hadn't changed. "I'm telling you what I know. Morrison had a meet just before they hit Moe's bar. Nobody bought the gay guys' solicitation bit, but that guy, the leather smith, did deal a fair amount of drugs when he lived in the Haight. The way Morrison laid it out was that by jumping this guy, it would send a signal to anybody else that the Malloy wasn't going to be the next Haight, and they should back off. The other stuff, well, citizens sometimes take it in the ear when we're trying to show

144

presence. We didn't do anything illegal, just made it loud and clear that we were around. That's how we started moving 'em out in the Haight, you remember that? In somebody's face." He lit another cigarette and glanced over at the girl in the booth who, in the whirling lights, looked like just a thin cloud of blue smoke."

"I know you're just giving me the message from above, but my gut says it's phony."

"I'm not disagreeing, but I still got 10 years to early retirement and, unlike you, can't put a good sentence together."

"All right, let's assume that's the scenario. What about Natasha, my neighbor's granddaughter?"

Jake finished his drink and motioned for another. "You're pushin' the envelope, Mike. You don't want to go there."

"I know, but I am, Jake."

"Damn. You're gonna laugh at me but, again, it's all I know. The old Russian owned a tannery in the industrial area of Detroit. He did some custom work for two or three of the big car companies and jobs for very rich people. A few years ago, a guy wants his motorhome done with the best leather, and no price is too high. The only catch is that this guy wants the Russian himself to do the install out at this guy's estate in some fancy suburb. He's working on the thing. There's a shooting. He sees it, but nobody remembers

Strings   *Roger Simpson*

he's hanging around, because the garages are across a huge lawn away from the house. He keeps working, and an hour later the guy comes out to see how the Russian is doing. He's very pleased, and casually asks the Russian how's it going and leaves. The old man keeps coming to work scared shitless as if he knows nothing, and a week later finishes the job and goes straight to the police. The guy was like Mr. Numero Uno in the heroin trade, it turns out, and the old man's testimony seals him for twenty years. He gets out in five. Thus, the two in the Mustang."

"After old Mr. Dobkovnic? That's gotta be pure fantasy. Professionals don't miss and kill a child in the bargain."

"All I can tell you." Mike put down a tip but Jake put it back in Mike's coat pocket. "Good to see you. Sorry if it doesn't work for you."

"Thanks for trying. Maybe you're right." Mike got off the stool just as two very large SID cops strolled in. One picked up some peanuts from a bar dish, and as they wandered through the tables to the booth where the girl was he chucked some at the blonde on the platform, hitting her undulating breasts. Her face went suddenly hard, then immediately back to its stone smile and she spun around and started moving her ass like her breasts. The two broke up with laugher, almost falling on a group of tourists who had four tables pushed together.

146

"My guys." Jake laughed. "Oh. There's nothing out there worth looking for, Mike. Trust me. In a few weeks, I'm sure Morrison will call this off and things will get normal again." Mike shook his hand and headed for the red curtains. The blonde was facing forward again.

The night was cool but not chilly. He left the van and walked further down to the many steps that led up from Kearney onto Telegraph Hill. After the heavy air of the bar, he wanted the exercise. It grew more quiet and darker as he climbed until he reached Jon Lee's street and came around the side of the hill that faced the bay and Marin County. He lived in a duplex, and had rented the two-bedroom lower half for several years from the elderly couple above who'd eventually asked if he would like to buy it in a condo conversion. Now it was his, and as Mike walked down the dark path, he could feel the hint of Jon Lee in the rustle of a breeze in bamboo and the bonsais, a cedar and a cypress, sitting by the thick, weathered front door Jon Lee had installed. He rang. No sound. He walked back up the path. Where would he be? He was a homebody.

At the top of the stairs he saw a light go on and an upstairs window open. "Hello?" A voice spoke in the darkness.

"It's Jon Lee's friend, Mike Hamilton, Mr. Kroneberger. I was looking for him."

147

His wife appeared behind him as he spoke. "Oh, Mike. Just checking. Don't know where Jon Lee is. Hasn't been home all day. Not like him."

"If you happen to see him would you ask him to call me?"

"Sure, Mike. Night." The window closed and the light went out.

By the time he got back down the hill, the fresh night air had cleared his lungs and he felt relaxed. For old time's sake, he was going to stop for an espresso at the Trieste, but when he got to the door he changed his mind and continued up to the van.

A thick fog had come over the darkness by the time he got home, and it muffled the usual city noises, making it almost as still as a forest or desert. There was no note on his door or in his box from Anna. Jon Lee hadn't called. Where was he? As he lay back on the bed, he hoped he didn't know the answer to that. It wouldn't let him sleep, but what could he do?

He didn't have a clue, and lay awake until nearly one o'clock before he fitfully drifted off to sleep. At five-thirty, the phone startled him. "Hello."

"Hey, honorable Mike-san. It's me."

"Where are you?"

"Oakland, California. Been sleeping in the Porsche all night. Wouldn't recommend it. The *Noodle man* delivered."

"What are you going to do? Maybe I shouldn't ask if you're grandstanding on this."

"Naw. The driver is camped out at a sleazebag motel out off Jack London Square. Very raw. You know the network. This guy was in the Tenderloin, and figured after what happened he'd better find new accommodations. They keep tabs on guys like this, don't ask me how or why but *Noodle man* made a dozen calls and I'm here on the dark side of the bay. Hang on." Jon Lee put the phone down and Mike could hear the sound of a foghorn through it. "Light just went on in Room 6, our boy. I need to stay sharp now."

"Wait a minute! Wait for me or call in some help."

"I don't need that kind of help. Here's my last bulletin, *Noodle man* says the chief's calling those Malloy incidents himself, except for the little girl."

"What? That can't be."

"I just need to follow the twine and see where this guy goes."

"My bet it's to the money he hasn't collected yet."

"You think pretty good for a white boy. If you don't hear from me by noon, you can call somebody you trust."

"Wait, Jon Lee…" But the phone went silent.

Jon Lee watched the door of Room 6 across the street. Only the garbage trucks and a street sweeper were out this early except for an occasional ring of the bell in an all-night gas station nearby when somebody drove in. At seven, the light went out. He waited, two, three, four minutes, but the door remained closed. He fired up the Porsche and hung a U, parking directly in front of the motel.

Still nothing for almost another five minutes, when the man finally emerged with a red duffel bag hung over his shoulder. Jon Lee lowered his head until the man was a block away, then he got out of the car. Jon Lee was dressed in the white outfit of a Chinese laundryman and he carried a bundle of white towels tied both ways with string. The bamboo staff was hidden against his body by the towels.

The driver was skinny and about 5'7". He wore jeans, grey and blue hiking boots, a blue polo shirt and one of those phony weathered leather jackets. They were going deeper into the pier district toward the docks, and the fog still hung thinly around the warehouse roofs. The man kept checking street signs until he found his, and walked three blocks until it ended in the piers where longshoremen were standing in small circles talking, drinking coffee and smoking, awaiting the call from inside a small brick building for that day's assignment. Across the broad street, and right on the waterfront, was a long two-story building with large round windows on both floors. It appeared to have been completely restored to its 1900's architectural grandeur, even down to the gold leaf paint. In the center were steps and a broad entry, above which was a hand-carved, ornate sign, also in gold leaf that said, "Locke and Neilson, Construction and Shipping." At the left side was an opening big enough to drive a semi through. It appeared to be a garage entrance, and was covered by a corrugated metal door. The hitman seemed uncertain what to do next. Turning away from the street he bent down and adjusted his pants and socks, and Jon Lee figured he had a small caliber weapon in an ankle holster. Then he crossed the street, hands in pockets, went up the stairs and rang a bell. The door buzzed and he was inside. Jon Lee checked his watch. 6:58. He followed.

Jon Lee presumed cameras, at least at the front door, but found none around the garage entrance. He went up the steps and looked inside. The glass was tinted so he couldn't see anything but his own image. Suddenly the door opened, and a man about sixty in a blue jacket with a badge emblem on it and wearing a watch cap with the same emblem stepped out. He had a large gun in a hip holster. "What the hell you looking in here for, Chinaman?"

Jon Lee contorted his face into a grimace. "Oh, so solly, so solly. This 'rong place. I make delivery." He smiled idiotically. "So solly. Even wrong rock."

The man looked at him in disgust. "Well, beat it. We do our own laundry." He closed the door and Jon

151

Lee went down the steps along the building and past the big garage entrance and into the wide alley to the right of that which led back to the piers. But the building was like a fortress back there with no windows at ground level, and those above were covered with decorative wrought iron. There was a double door of steel with no exterior handles at pier level. The garage door was his only possible entry. The building was located near the end of the piers, and since it was Saturday there were few if any passing cars. The corrugated door was much thicker than most, and was set back about ten feet inside the building so unless someone was looking, Jon Lee went unnoticed.

He set the towels aside and tried the door. There was less than a three-inch play in it, but that was enough to wedge his staff under it. Hunched down with his feet squarely on the ground, he closed his eyes and quieted his breath until he had channeled all his energy into his arms and legs. This had been part of his 12th Circle Mastery training, except here there was no time for contemplation. Then he could sense it before it happened; there was a grinding and a snap of metal, like two heavy objects hitting each other. He moved, still crouched with the bamboo, to the center of the garage and applied the same pressure until there was another snap. He could only hope no one heard it as he returned to his original location, and pushed his fingers under the strings so the towels hung to his wrist as he wedged that side of the door up and rolled under it just as it fell back into place.

He was in semi-darkness going down a ramp that led into a basement that must have covered the entire length and breadth of the building. On the front wall were partially lit offices with large glass windows looking onto the open area which contained tractors, dump trucks and skip loaders of all sizes and neatly parked in marked slots. On the back wall were a series of mechanic's bays with other heavy construction equipment in various stages of maintenance and repair. He darted from shadow to shadow until he saw the stairs. On the first landing, he peered out through a small window into the lobby where floors and columns were made of grey marble. Away from the front door was a desk where the security guard was sitting. He had his head turned away from the door, and was watching Saturday morning cartoons on a small television on another table. Jon Lee presumed that there was an elevator directly to his right next to a staircase. He began to climb. Before he reached the second landing, he heard muffled voices.

"I told you. I'm not going on any rides. The deal was you meet me at the motel at noon in the parking lot. You show me the money. I take it. You drive off. End of contract."

Jon Lee opened the stairwell door and was in another lobby. The walls were paneled in cherry wood.

153

One side was a double door with brass plate letters, *Locke-Neilson Shipping Company*, and on the opposite side of the lobby across a thick beige rug there were identical doors reading, *Locke-Neilson Construction Company*. One of those doors was ajar, and Jon Lee moved closer to it. He was barely able to see through the crack, but it was wide enough to configure the room.

There was another lobby, and the voices were coming from an office on the other side whose double doors were both slightly ajar. High windows also encased in thick cherry wood frames ran the length of the room. He sensed the lobby was empty, and gracefully moved around the front door and across a large oriental rug covering most of an oak plank floor. This was obviously a secretary's office, from the French writing desk to one side and a series of chairs, a fax machine and a coffee table. On the wall behind the desk were two portraits, one of a very stout red-faced man in his sixties dressed in blue jeans and a plaid wool red shirt. He had on a yellow hard hat. The other man was dressed in sailing attire, white slacks and a thick, ribbed turtle neck sweater. Jon Lee recognized Charles Locke.

"Mr. Johnson, do you really think you're in any position to set the terms at this point, the way you and your buddy fucked this up?" The room had a bank of the same high, broad windows in thick cherry wood frames that looked out on the piers and the bay. The man talking was sitting on the front of a Baroque carved walnut desk. There was a drafting table behind it and some chairs in front, with a bookcase along the far wall. The hitman was leaning against one of the chairs. There was another man dressed for golf with massive arms and chest who leaned against the bookcase. Two others, both dressed in sports coats and open collar, button-down shirts sat in the chairs furthest from Johnson with their legs crossed, staring at him.

"I'm not that stupid. People back home don't get a call from me, from my house in Jersey by tomorrow midnight, they'll be looking for me and they got your address, and they aren't as polite as me."

The big man by the bookcase pushed himself away and stood erect. He stuck his finger in his nose like he was picking and itching it at the same time. "This guy is smart, Bob," he said to the one on the desk who slid off and walked closer to the hitman.

Bob looked over at the golfer. "You're right, Johnny. We had him figured wrong." The golfer's arm flashed out and a fist connected deep into the hitman's stomach. He let out a groan and fell to his knees, gasping for breath.

The big man came around the chair, yanked the hitman's legs out so he was flat on the floor and came down with his knees on the man's back. He searched him and found the gun. "He really is a smart guy." The two in the chairs hadn't moved, but they laughed.

Beyond the door, Jon Lee pretended to be spellbound by what was happening but he had heard the footsteps on the stairs and fully anticipated the cold barrel of the gun on his neck. "Move or I'll blow you back to China, you gook bastard! Walk!" The aging security guard shoved him against the double doors and they flew open.

"What the hell is this!?"

"He came to the front door, Bob. Said he was delivering these towels."

The golfer walked over and grabbed Jon Lee by the throat. "How the hell did you get in here laundry boy? You can't even open that gate with the biggest skip loader we got when it's out of order."

Jon Lee, with the towels still hanging to his wrist, held his arms high in the air, his eyes bugged out with terror. "I come through big door right here in front. Me think different company there!" The big man let go and pushed Jon Lee into the empty chair.

"Which of you numb nuts forgot to close it? What's that stick?" he asked Jon Lee.

"Oh, nothing, always carry since come from China. Good ruck rike labbit's foot."

Everyone seemed to smile at once. They pulled Johnson up and slammed him into a chair just as the phone rang. Robert picked it up. "Yes. Yes, sir. We've got him. Yes, sir." He hung up. "He's docking on the other side of the wharf, just for precaution, in about forty-five minutes. Tom, take the car over and pick him up." He motioned to the security guard. "Good work, Marty. Now go get us some sweet rolls and coffee from the bakery if it's open." The guard left.

The golfer got down in front of the slumped over hitman and picked up the ankle with the holster attached. "I better just take that from you." He jerked the leg and the bone cracked as Johnson screamed in pain. "Now, it won't hurt so much if you're real still."

The one remaining in the chairs uncrossed his legs. "What about this Chinese?"

They all looked at Jon Lee whose face was filled with agony and fear. "Please, I good boy. Work hard. Make mistake only." He had set the towels on the floor. His staff was resting in the chair to his right.

"Better wait and see what Mr. Locke says," the one in the chair offered.

Bob nodded. "Sit tight, laundry boy." He motioned to the golfer as the security guard reappeared about ten minutes later with hot cinnamon rolls and big coffees and set it down on a table by the window next to the drafting table and went back down stairs. "Mr. Locke wants to be sure he doesn't forget the plans in that leather tube by the bookcase. He's taking them to his safe in the Union Street office." The golfer picked it up and touched it to his forehead as if he was saluting with it. They gathered around the coffee and rolls on the big desk.

Jon Lee stood up. "Cold coffee this morning, boys," he said in his normal voice and the bamboo staff was airborne. It caught Bob against the side of his head directly on his temple and his neck twisted back as if he'd been shot. The staff hit the frame of one of the windows and went dead center into the forehead of the one who'd been in the chair. As it fell to the floor, Jon Lee caught it and twirled out of the grip of the golfer and to the other end of the Oriental rug by the doors.

The big man spread his arms and hurled himself at Jon Lee whom he outweighed by a good seventy-five pounds. It was like a linebacker ready to sack a quarterback. Jon Lee didn't move, and all the false fear earlier on his face had gone. When the big man was a foot away, in a single motion, Jon Lee grabbed his collar, knelt and hurled him through the double doors and into the secretary's office. He came down hard on the back of his neck, rolled over and back up like a leaf turning in the gutter, and smashed with his whole body into the second set of double doors before he fell backward onto the carpet and lay still.

Jon Lee calculated that there was less than ten minutes before Locke would be there, and he quickly surveyed the room. There was nothing obvious but the leather case and he pulled out the plans inside. It was just a single sheet which appeared to be part of a full set. It was in standard blueprint blue ink, the drawing of the lower level garage, but drafted in pencil in a space where there'd been nothing before was what looked like a passage with three offshoots, one ending in a box-like room. It meant nothing to him, probably last minute changes, and he put it back in the leather case and left it where it had been on the desk. The hitman had passed out, and his pulse was erratic, his breathing shallow. He couldn't carry him. His karma was coming for him. Jon Lee took one quick look around, but there was nothing.

On the first landing, the guard was back at the television, and Jon Lee decided to exit as he'd entered. But as he raced up the ramp he heard the squeak and drag of something half broken trying to work. A Chrysler Town car with deeply tinted windows was coming down the ramp. As it passed him, he raced to the exit where the broken door was descending again, and Jon Lee vanished into the Oakland Saturday morning.

Chapter Eleven

"What is this parasite before us? A monk, a beggar, a sniveler who lights candles and offers prayers to dead gods? The warlord strode onto the overhang followed by a small company of his men and stopped a spear's length from the monk. "Where are the fools from the village below? They could hide nothing from me. But their attempt will prolong the pain of their deaths. I am Khilma! Where are those villagers, insect? Tell me and I may spare you to serve in my tent."

He had been worried during the entire trip on his second visit that Esse would be furious about the death of the little girl. Designate 8 had witnessed just a hint of that anger and it still unnerved him. Instead, Esse had been both compassionate and philosophical. He too had known such sorrow because his first born had been accidentally killed by British gunfire. His heart went out to the parents. Designate 8 was about to tell him that it had been the straw that made the Russians decide to sell and move further north to the wine country where their son had found new work after selling the tannery in Detroit. But Esse had just smiled and said, "I know, I know, my friend. And those two queer men have done the same."

This startled Designate 8. How could he have known? But he said nothing. "I never doubted that we would accomplish this. We are on the side of peace. And thanks to your fine efforts in getting the plans pushed through the red tape we begin our construction, even without the last house. But, I can assure you that like the others, they will sell too." He laughed. "Once they are covered with dust each day." He rose and motioned for Designate 8 to do the same. "This day I have gathered all the designates from around the world to my city because I want to share with all of you the power of our vision. Come, we go to our new amphitheater, especially constructed for the demonstration." The wall opened and they went into the corridor.

Although the Huntington Hotel on Nob Hill was as refined and beautiful as any Dama had visited in other large cities of the world, she had been cooped up there for nearly three days now without going out. Rasheed and the technicians had no trouble setting up Panjali's "magic" briefcase, and were assured that the five-interconnecting room suite they occupied on the top floor was secure. Everything was in place and she

161

had already made three successful transmissions to her father. It was strange seeing him on the little screen, and she already missed him badly. Though he had never had the advantages he had given Abyase and her, in raising them he'd managed to transcend many of the old-fashioned ways of his ancestors. As busy as he became by the time she was six, there was never a day they didn't spend some time together. One of the things she loved was just the two of them taking long walks beyond the confines of the city which had been finished the day before her twelfth birthday.

He would guide her out beyond the underground storage and warehouse facilities, beyond the water purification plant and the place she called "the deep hum" that powered everything. Here the corridor lights ended and one had to walk with a gas torch or flashlights through what seemed a maze of earthen tunnels that were not much taller than a man's height and very narrow. He made her memorize the correct ways to turn and which passage--right, left or center— she must take both leaving and entering the holy city through the secret door deep in the desert. Sometimes she grew impatient and even a little fearful that she might be lost, clinging to his hand. But always the passage would come to an end where the iron stairs went steeply upward. He'd press the back of his hand on a blue light that was behind a thick glass on the wall, and suddenly the whoosh would come and then the click and the sound of a soccer ball being deflated. Then the light of the desert and a thin mist of sand would cover them as they climbed through what she always thought of as the hatch to a submarine where they would be embraced by the silence of the desert. Her father would close the hatch, and a breeze from nowhere would cover it with sand.

They always brought a lunch, and would walk through the utter silence and heat for about a mile until they came to a small oasis with a pond, a well, and a water tower about fifty yards away and down the other side of a dune where it stood its lonely watch. It was as if it was waiting for the old steam-powered trains that still came this way carrying people and supplies from Mecca and back to one of the most distant mines and nearly depleted oil fields, the first that had been drilled in the country. She never knew what they mined there, but it couldn't have been very valuable since the train was the only way to get there. She would pretend to be his servant, and politely and delicately lay out a mat and arrange the food and water for their picnic.

That had truly been their special place. He told stories of her ancestors and their pride and challenges, and she would talk about her friends in the holy city or work that her tutor made her do that she didn't want to do. When she would come home for vacations from England, they would go there and even today she still shared her doubts and fears with him there. She would ask his advice about men she had met, and his perceptions were uncanny. There were times of dark moments of self-doubt that she wondered if she would ever find a man who would affirm her independence of thought rather than shy away from it. Sometimes she felt as if she had an invisible shield surrounding her, like she was locked in a castle tower.

Twice, men who she found sensitive and caring finally departed, telling her they felt their own insecurities did not allow a relationship. Her father had pondered that on one of their oasis visits and looked deeply into her eyes. "Be open, my Dama. You are unique, and I believe that will eventually magnetize someone as equally unique in his own right. But it is hard to be patient, isn't it?" There was nothing she couldn't share with him as they sat eating quietly.

And the same pattern of returning to the opening would occur, only then she could see that there was pain in his hand which grew worse the closer they got to the top of the dune where the hatch was. This was a dune that would never shift. Finally, he would find the spot, and push away the sand to reveal the same blue light covered by thick glass. He touched it with the back of his hand and moved away as the whooshing began and it popped up. Then he would make her find the way back through the tunnels until they came into a corridor and the warehouse area. Though she didn't know why, she knew it was right when the same microscopic device was imbedded in her hand when she was sixteen.

She glanced out the window. A cable car bell rang below as it rumbled past, and though it was only ten, several mothers and nannies played and strolled with small children in the grassy park in front of Grace Cathedral. Rasheed was reading the morning news in the long twenty-foot-high living room. She asked, "Do you want to take a walk with me? I feel like going to see the ocean."

He glanced up, rather doubtful. "Are you sure?"

"Rasheed, I've lived abroad and been on adventures far riskier than going to the shore."

"You wouldn't obey me anyway," he sighed. "Take Chaudri and Mohammed with you, of course."

"Of course. We may eat lunch at Fisherman's Wharf or somewhere, so don't expect us back until this afternoon."

"Be back for the evening report."

"I will. But with Designate 8 gone to the Holy City again, there's little to report. He seemed quite depressed this morning. Consider getting out for a little walk yourself."

"I'll go down to the gym here and take a swim."

She gathered the bodyguards and went out. In the underground garage, the chauffeur, hired from an exclusive security company, was waiting at the elevator area and she asked him to take them on a scenic route to the beach. They drove along California until the cable car line ended at Van Ness. The limousine zigzagged over a dozen streets fronted by apartments in various stages of repair and deterioration. They drove along the edge of the Filmore ghetto and a Panhandle where the trees appeared abruptly out of the flat landscape until they were driving through Golden Gate Park. The driver wasn't very talkative but managed to point out what he described as "where they grow hothouse plants," the Conservatory partway through the park. She asked him to drive to the furthest parking area and said they would meet him in the one closest to the park so she could get a mile or two of walking in.

There was a thick fog lying close to the sand and water, but it wasn't cold so she left her shoes in the car with her coat and set out with just a cotton turtle neck, black pleated pants and the thick red cloth belt she'd bought in the hotel shop. She loved the feeling of the sand, wet and dry, and rolled up her pants so she could walk in the dying fingers of surf rolling weakly onto the beach. Looking both ways, she couldn't see anyone but the bodyguards who, looking rather absurd in dark suits and white tennis shoes, meandered behind her at a respectful distance. In the dense fog, she felt the peace of actually being alone.

She looked forward to seeing all of San Francisco and was already bored with keeping track of Designate 8. But he was an interesting person who could use power equally well to defeat an enemy or help a friend. And his devotion to his poor wife was beyond question.

Her purpose had been to walk fast for exercise, but instead she lolled along just enjoying the coolness and the smell of ocean air. They'd probably gone no more than half a mile when she heard a sound coming from a place to her right where the dunes seemed to come together to form a crater between them. The sound was clearer as she walked the short distance to the opening between the dunes. It reminded her of someone breathing in a strange way, just like a yogi she had seen once in India. There was a quick inhale with a slow exhale, but there was no indication that whoever was doing it was straining.

Coming around the corner of the hill of sand, she discovered a man about six feet tall, thin but muscular with his shirt removed and wearing a pair of purple, baggy pants. He appeared to be moving in slow motion, and suddenly she had to catch her breath and knelt in the sand. It wasn't the fine whiteness of the Sahara. She felt a chill and embraced her breasts, holding her shoulders for warmth. But she couldn't take her eyes off the man who had begun to move faster and faster around the crater until he seemed a blur. Dama had no idea how long this went on, but suddenly he came to rest, bowed for no reason with his palms together and took a deep breath.

167

He smiled at her, said "Good Morning," and picked up a towel, a small brown leather fanny pack and a sweatshirt. He paused, hesitated, and then walked toward her.

"Hello," she stammered. "What were you doing?"

"Practicing…as I do every day here." He smiled again. "Rain or shine."

"You must be quite disciplined. I am too, but, perhaps not that much. What is this practice, if I may ask?" He was close now and his eyes would not leave hers.

"An ancient art both physical and spiritual." He reached out and took her hand, helping her up. "Some say the most ancient of its kind. There is only one true Master left in the line of Masters in the world. Mine." Jon Lee was still holding her hand and they looked down at it in unison and laughed. He slowly let go. "I…well, excuse me. I'm sorry."

"No, that's…your hand is so warm and I'm cold."

"Here, it's clean." He made her put on the sweatshirt.

"But you…you're dripping wet."

"I'll live, I'm sure." He toweled off and wrapped the towel around his neck.

Chaudri and Mohammed appeared in the opening between the dunes and were coming toward them when she waved them off. "I'm fine."

They came out onto the sand. The tide was still receding.

"Where do you go now?"

He motioned up the beach. "My car is parked up there. I usually run in the sand for a while now but, perhaps, I can walk with you. I assume that's where you're parked too?"

"Yes." They began to walk with the bodyguards fading back a discriminating distance though they both appeared concerned, talking to each other in Arabic.

"I've never seen you here. Do you live in the city?"

"No, I am just visiting. We are up at the Huntington Hotel."

"Very fancy. You must have lots of oil wells back home."

She laughed. "Why do you say that?"

"Well, you're from somewhere far away and I'll bet it's always very hot and dry and there's more sand than this." He glanced around.

"How did you know?" They were close now and Dama was feeling both nervous and calm. She had the impulse to take his hand again.

She was walking furthest from the sea and as he looked out at a series of small waves he glanced at her hair and face and, more dimly, at her body. "Your friends are speaking Arabic."

"I live some distance from Mecca."

"The princess from an oasis who has been well educated in western understanding."

She laughed. "My British accent?"

"Yes."

"That may be. but I think of myself as independent with a streak of the old-fashioned Arabic girl."

"That's a miracle. And tell me about your castle by the oasis?"

She hesitated. "A quiet place...with no oil wells in sight."

Jon Lee smiled and they walked on for almost a mile in silence. She felt completely at peace with him. The Cliff House restaurant was barely visible as the road climbed to it and they come to the edge of the parking lot. "Is that your car...and no oil wells?"

"My car."

She took off the sweatshirt. "Thank you. You're kind."

"I will probably never wash it."

"What? I don't understand."

"Oh, just American humor, not very funny I guess. Look, could I...may I call you? I'm with the police, a detective, and I know this city like the back of my hand. I'd love to show it to you." They were almost to the car and the driver held the door open.

"I don't know if that would be possible." She bit her lip. "I think it's impossible."

"I just want to show you the city." He took a card from the fanny pack. "Please, call me if you wish." She reached for it and their hands paused again for a second. Then she took it.

"Perhaps, I don't know. Goodbye." She got into the car.

"I hope not," he said to himself as he watched the limousine drive away.

They entered a room which had a circular corridor with a series of doors just a few feet apart. Designate 8 thought it odd to see standard sized doors in a place with such advanced technology. Esse bid him farewell and a young man about twenty escorted him down the passage. "This is your cubicle, sir. It has the best view. During the demonstration, to assure all the designates' identities remain secret, the door will be locked."

Designate 8 looked back anxiously as the boy gently shut the door and the lock clicked into place. He was in a very small room, just big enough for two or three people with a comfortable office swivel chair positioned toward a large glass window. A small ice box on his left held juice, scotch, crackers and cheese. His view was from the angle of a theatre balcony and looked down on a stage about twenty yards away. The curtain, the color and fabric of the oatmeal robes, was drawn shut and to the far right was a podium. He mixed a scotch, ate some cheese and crackers and checked his watch.

There was a copy of yesterday's *San Francisco Chronicle* on top of the refrigerator and he started thumbing through it. He'd just finished one story when a small man seemed to pop out from behind the curtain, waved and walked to the podium. He wore a white shirt, tan shorts and sandals and had a mass of unruly black hair. Designate 8 couldn't make eye contact from that distance.

"Good day to all of you, sirs. Welcome to the Holy City of Esse. I am called Panjali, the chief scientist who tries to keep the place running." Designate 8 laughed at that and he thought he heard laughter through the wall on his left. He assumed that all the designates, how many he had no idea, were each in a cubicle like his.

Panjali pointed at the curtains with his finger and they opened. On the stage were two cubicles that looked to be about twenty feet wide by fifteen high by ten deep. They were made either of glass or some

172

material that made all sides visible and they were joined together but separated by another wall of the same substance. The one on the right was a near exact replica of a portion of the financial district of San Francisco, but the windows of the buildings were open and dozens of white mice scurried along the streets, darted into buildings and sometimes poked their heads out of upper story windows. The section on the left was a beautiful urban scene with a magnificent looking English Tudor house with a backdrop of oaks and rolling hills. It was the rear of the house because there were beautifully tended gardens and pathways, a large stone patio and swimming pool. Dolls like those Barbie and Ken ones his granddaughters played with were positioned as if at a barbeque party. A few sat by the pool on lounges, some dangled their feet and others were in the water. Several gathered around tables with deep green umbrellas adjacent to the red brick barbeque that was smoking and had what looked like a large rib roast and two chickens on dual revolving spits.

"I wish to impress upon all of you that what you are about to see is utterly unthinkable on our road to world peace together. But let it be a reminder of the power that each of you represent to those in the world who wish to keep us all in an unnatural state of anxiety and ongoing war. We want you to leave here today confident that such purveyors of greed and satanic hedonism are no match for peace and those who follow

Esse's road to that goal in the not very distant future."
He paused and seemed to be considering each glass
partitioned cubicle, and Designate 8 looked away as
Panjali's gaze fell upon him. Then he smiled again and
clapped his hands, walked around the podium and,
pointing to the side with the mice said, "Keep your eyes
on our little friends. And don't worry, they will not be
harmed."

Suddenly and without a sound the buildings
began to crumble, sending the mice in all directions.
Back and forth they raced near the front windows as
each building fell and a fine dust rose from where they
stood. The creatures remained pressed against the
windows, seemingly in terror, but they appeared to be
fine. "In our Holy City, no mice are harmed and none
are ever experimented upon. The little rascals are just
fine." He laughed. "You get the point, yes, a power
that can eliminate inorganic matter while not harming
mice…or people. Now, observe the happy garden party,
and remember that these figures have a molecular
structure that is almost human."

The hair on the back of his neck was standing
up as Designate 8 thought of the implications of this,
but he had not in his wildest imagination anticipated
what happened next. It seemed to creep into that soft
urban setting because, again, there was not a sound. But
some unknown and deadly source had caused the dolls
to begin to melt as if they were being burned alive from

174

within. Faces turned to fluid, a slow-moving lava, as they disintegrated, running down over bare chests and bikini breasts which caused the dolls to fall forward into the barbeque pit, against chairs, onto the lawn, into each other and the pool. Then, it stopped and before Designate 8 was the remainder of arms, partial faces and heads, legs, and clothing half buried in what would have been burning flesh.

The twitch was returning to his face and he took a large swallow of the scotch, and then another. When he looked back, he saw Panjali emerge grinning from ear to ear from behind the backdrop of green rolling hills. "As you see, just seconds after, it is perfectly safe for me. And, as you see, not so much as an umbrella damaged. He climbed over the house and gently nudged what was left of a young girl into the pool. Her form sizzled and smoked as it touched the water and disappeared beneath.

Designate 8 felt as if he would throw up as he stumbled in the direction he thought was the door. The last thing he remembered before passing out was the utter, horrifying silence through all that crumbling destruction of buildings and the doll by the pool, its steaming body dissolving into the blue water.

Chapter Twelve

At the first sight of the warlord, fear had sprung back into Wo Chin; the man's face, its creases filled with dry dirt, ash and blood. The long bulbous nose reminded him of a demon temple carving. A ragged beard hung down over his massive chest. But the memory of what he had just done with the rock arose as well and consumed the fear. When he spoke, his voice was strong, as if someone else was speaking.

'The people of Wang Ny are in my monastery, up the path behind that rock.'

'And did you and your brother maggots push that rock to block my path?'

'My brothers are on a pilgrimage to the Shrine of Light on the high peak.'

'Oh, and they left you to defend these villagers against my wrath?' The warlord and his men roared with laughter.

Chief McGrady had a Butterfinger in his mouth and was consuming it like a frog would a large insect when Charles Locke called for the fourth time in two days. He picked up the phone and held it slightly away from his ear in anticipation of another diatribe.

"Well?"

"Charles, I already told you. This must be done with kid-gloves. Oakland is out of my jurisdiction and I can't just go barging in on Ted Sorensen's territory."

"I can't believe that you don't have any other contacts."

But in all his years of police work, McGrady had never cultivated any underworld contacts. "Well, I just don't."

"Christ, I would have gotten more results by now. You've got my employees who've given you a description—Oriental about six feet with fairly long hair, and he obviously wasn't a Chinese laundry boy, given that he had to have broken into my offices. And what about the baseball bat or whatever he was carrying. The biggest of my three men won't be out of the hospital for a least another three weeks."

"I know, I know. Just give me a little more time." Locke hung up without saying goodbye and McGrady took the Butterfinger out of his ashtray and stuck it back between his lips. He got up and walked to the windows and thought about the vineyard. Then he began to pace, but the phone rang again. He looked dumbly over at it and continued to pace until his secretary spoke through the intercom, "It's Captain Morrison, sir."

"Okay, okay, I got it." He plopped back down in his heavily padded leather desk chair and answered. "Yeah, Morey, what's up? I hope not more problems."

"No, but I got to thinking. I didn't want to say anything when you first asked because it's so farfetched. You know the guy who broke into that big developer's office?"

"What do you mean?"

"There's a guy over in Homicide. I think he's a Jap. Name's Koshima. He's the one who ran down those two who killed the little girl."

"Come on, Morey, a cop?"

"Yeah, and a damn good one. Joe Alston, his boss, says he's the best he's got but he's odd, keeps to himself and, here's the really odd part, he carries a gun but apparently never uses it, and he's been on lots of flaky assignments."

"So what?"

"He's into one of the martial arts. Joe said his record showed that when he went through the academy he refused to do hand-to-hand until he was forced to. After that, they excused him because even the black belt, who's the chief instructor, couldn't touch him, and got hurt trying. My point is, the reason he's a little wacko is because he carries this…it's not a baseball bat or like that. It's a sort of stick, maybe fifteen inches long and a couple inches around. I know it sounds stupid, but I know Koshima has been in trouble for taking things into his own hands before. You remember about ten, maybe twelve years ago, it was in the paper. That bank standoff with hostages down at Market and Montgomery? SWAT teams knee deep, the streets blocked, and suddenly around the corner comes this guy dressed in laundry whites carrying a bundle of towels. He's acting totally oblivious to fifty cops shouting at him and goes right to the bank door and knocks. Big smile the whole time. Then he gets pulled inside."

"Yeah, yeah, sure. I was down there. Looked like one dumb sonofabitch."

"And five minutes later he's on the phone, telling us the four guys inside are subdued and it's okay to come in. And he was just a rookie then! Look, I know you think I'm nuts but the MO is almost identical except the baseball bat part."

"You could be right, Morey, thanks for the info." He hung up and walked to the door and leaned into the reception area. "Kathy, would you call personnel and have them send me over a picture of Lieutenant Jon Lee Koshima? He's in Homicide."

That same evening Mike arrived at Kishu's on Union Street down in the Marina District. He'd liked the area better before they'd begun yuppifying the old storefronts, but the restaurant had seen lots of changes in the thirty years it had been there.

Even on a week night, the bar and front lobby were standing room only. He made his way to where the hostess usually stood. Just as he was about to give her his name, a Japanese man about half a head taller than himself with his hair combed back in a long knotted ponytail suddenly appeared at his side and took his arm. "I always save tables for Pulitzer winners." They shook hands. "Come on, Mike, he's already here"

He followed Tad Kishu, who had taken over the restaurant from his father, into the main dining area. It was composed of a deck that surrounded a Koi pond and tropical garden upon which mist periodically fell from the ceiling. Around the deck were a series of private rooms, probably two dozen, each with shoji screen sliding doors whose panels had been copied from originals in Japanese temples. There was another section beyond this with actual tables, but the private rooms were prized and not necessarily awarded to the same people each time they came. It was Tad's way of keeping even the powerful humble.

"He's in good spirits for a change."

"You've noticed too."

"Too many nights on a bar stool here lately, but he's suddenly not drinking." He volunteered, "Did he tell you that he met somebody?"

"No kidding. That's fantastic."

"But better not press the issue. You know how he is."

"Do I ever. Almost ten years in a squad car together. I won't say a word."

He led Mike to the last room on the far side. Jon Lee was already seated cross-legged at the low lacquered table, and Mike was glad to see that he was drinking a Pepsi, not sake. Tad smiled at Mike as he sat down. "Make sure this guy doesn't use that weird stick of his around here, will you?"

"I will if you can get somebody to deliver pronto a bottle of your best Japanese beer."

"Budweiser?"

"Get outta here." Mike waved him away.

"He never rests," Jon Lee said. "Seven days a week."

"You guys go back to high school?"

"Yes. This place is a close second in cleanliness behind those former pet store owners out your way. This is the cleanest restaurant, and I think tastiest, in the city."

"So?"

"Nothing. Just that one sheet of drafting paper with the odd addition. You find anything?" The kimono clad waitress entered, knelt and set down the beer and poured it, then rose. Jon Lee ordered in Japanese and she quietly closed the shoji.

181

"I hope you ordered something I can eat." Mike joked. "Well, I'll have to report zero as well, except Sue in the mayor's office says that it was Shelia Vernin who orchestrated the passaging of the Corfu project. It's done now so I doubt if Sue'll be able to help us further." They sat in silence for a moment as Jon Lee drank some Pepsi and Mike sipped the beer. Jon Lee looked at Mike. "Oh, no. I don't like that look."

"We need a second look, Mike, and you know it. I know they took the leather tube with the drawing to Locke's office which is only three blocks down from here. The one guy said something about putting it away in a safe there. Well, it couldn't be the wall variety, given the size of the tube."

"Okay, boy-san," Mike paused, "but I'm pretty old for this kind of stuff."

"Forty-two isn't old."

"I'll go on one condition."

"Shoot."

"If we come up with something we go see Carney, no joke."

"Why?"

"You know why, tie the strings together so far. You've got Locke, the Corfu Project, Shelia Vernin, the SID with a possible Chief McGrady connection. This can't all be coincidence."

"You're right."

"That's why the DA's office needs to know. I've known Carney since he was an assistant DA hired out of Hastings and I was a patrolman. You know he's discrete."

"You really think all this ties together?

Jon Lee reflected for a moment as the shoji opened and their dinner arrived.

"The logic's there. But where's the proof? We may soon see, won't we?" Mike smiled.

There seemed to be watery shapes above, as if he was looking up from beneath the waters of a swimming pool. They weren't moving much as if waiting for him. Designate 8's head and right shoulder ached. Then the water moved away slowly, and they took form. Esse was kneeling over him with two others behind dressed in white robes and carrying what looked like a green tool box. He started to panic when he suddenly realized that he was still in the cubicle, but Esse touched his arm and the ones in white helped him slowly to his feet and into the chair. "You frightened us, my friend."

"I...sorry. I blacked out."

"Yes, and then fell quite hard against that shoulder." Esse touched it very gently. "We've given you a shot that will heal it before you return home.

183

Luckily, nothing was broken." Esse took a delicate ceramic, blue cup from the others and had Designate 8 drink it all. "Nothing but herbs, sir, but concocted in such a special way. Far better than any of your western pharmaceutical poisons. Just rest for a moment." He nodded to the attendants and they left the two of them alone.

Designate 8 was amazed how quickly he felt normal again. It couldn't have been more than two or three minutes. "That demonstration was hard to watch."

"I know, especially since the texture of those dolls is as close to being human as can possibly be imagined. But remember Panjali's words? This power is only to demonstrate to those who want to continue taking their profits from wars that those days have ended."

"I understand."

"Come, I will walk you to your quarters. The liquid I gave you will give you a very restful sleep." When they entered Designates 8's "home," the mantle clock said 9:20. Esse sat down in one of the chairs by the empty fireplace and motioned him into the other one. "I believe that now I can completely trust you, while all the other Designates are still under investigation. Therefore, I want to share something so secret that even the Congress knows nothing about it, because it shows just how certain people in power will not be satisfied until no life exists on this planet, even if they must die in the process too. Are you familiar with a place somewhat east of what is called Kennedy Meadows?"

"Sure, it's in the Sierras. I've been through there several times. Beautiful."

"Your Pentagon, without any Congressional or Executive knowledge or approval has created an underground facility much like the one at your Cheyenne Mountain."

"That place is huge. That's the heart of everything for our defense."

"Well, the Kennedy Meadows facility is just the opposite. When it is finished, it will have an offensive missile capability of reaching any target on the globe except Antarctica."

"My God."

"Even the missile assembly will take place there. The silos are drilled upward from within but leaving the natural terrain untouched until there is a launch, and then the ground above is blown clear just before a launch. It's virtually undetectable."

"Yet, how is it that you know about it and are telling me?"

"As I said, I trust you and you must trust me regarding my sources and network of information. Do you?"

"Yes."

"Good. Sleep now. You will return to San Francisco tomorrow." Esse motioned him to remain seated and walked to the wall. As it slid back he turned to Designate 8. "On your next visit, we will discuss the United Nations *Week of Peace* and what your part will be."

"Where you're the main speaker?"

"Like this Kennedy Meadow, that information at the moment is just for your ears." Esse smiled and walked out. Designate 8 went immediately to the bar and carried the scotch back to the chair where he spread a throw blanket over himself and put his feet on the ottoman. He planned to slowly sip the whiskey, but he was asleep after two sips.

Chaudri and Mohammed both smiled at Dama when she said she wanted to walk on the beach again, but she tried to ignore it. Why shouldn't she enjoy the breeze? It was a crystal-clear day just cool enough for a light sweater. She'd even considered putting on some make-up but chastised herself for such foolishness. Her lashes and eye brows couldn't be any darker and the one time she'd had make-up applied to her face in London she burst out laughing; she had looked like a clown. She had deep olive skin. She was what she was.

She walked quickly up the beach. It was almost the exact time as before and she could hear him breathing behind the dune. She hesitated. Chaudri and Mohammed were laughing at a distance and she irritably motioned for them to be quiet. Finally, she walked softly forward. He had finished and was toweling off. He said, "Hi," as if he knew she would be coming.

"Hello. You're finished."

"Well, I had to be. I knew you were coming. Or should I say I've been hoping for days that you would come again."

"Me too."

He put his lips to his finger tips and touched her hand. "Are we going to walk again?"

"I guess so."

They walked on without a word. He could feel her presence so near him, but it was more than physical. It was like coming in after a hard workout, showering and sitting in the hot tub on his deck. "How is your visit coming along?"

"Oh, sometimes fine, sometimes very boring."

"You'd fall in love with the city if I showed it to you."

"I'm sure I would."

"Why can't we. You can bring those guys with you if you want."

"Really?"

"Sure. They'd probably enjoy it to."

But she shook her head just as they reached the parking lot. Then she stopped and looked partially at him and the sea. "Maybe. I have your card. Goodbye." She walked to the limousine.

"We don't even know each other's names." He called after her.

She turned back, still walking. "Dama."

"That's beautiful…Dama. I'm Jon Lee. And, please, stop saying goodbye."

The same night Jon Lee and Mike had dinner, Chief McGrady was struggling to get through another goddamned opera performance. His wife was always dragging him to this crap when he'd rather have been curled up in the den with a fire going and a good cop show or ball game on TV.

As usual, he'd pigged out at dinner in the opera dining room which had been given for some old fart about two hundred years old that droned on so long afterwards he thought they'd never get to the opera on time, even though it was just upstairs. The old guy was a foreign diplomat, had spent a long time at the UN and was on the organizing committee for the UN *Week of Peace* celebration coming up in a few months. That would be another pain in the ass, trying to figure how to

188

meet budget and pay all the overtime for security during that week.

He tried to focus his opera glasses on a big-breasted girl in a short red and white skirt and blouse with great legs and hair like white gold that must have hung down to her waist. He'd just settled back to enjoy this when a valet interrupted, telling him he had an important call in the lobby. He went into the VIP phone room and closed the door, sitting down in a stiff yellow arm chair. "McGrady."

"Evening, Chief. Having your usual fun at the opera?" Charles Locke sounded in good spirits which had been rare since the break-in.

"How come you're not here?"

"I hate the opera too, but don't tell anyone. I told my wife I had business so she went with our oldest daughter and her husband."

"Well, what's up?"

"All of my men positively identified your Lieutenant Koshima as the so-called laundry boy. No doubt."

"I can't figure why he'd be following the hitman. He's not even on that case."

"Nor I. And that is a big concern."

The little girl's face in the paper suddenly came to him. "Look, that's good. Now I'll handle it internally. I've had to fire lots of guys over the years. I know how a good frame-up works. He'll be looking for a job in two months."

"No, Chief."

"Look, Charles," he interrupted.

"I'm no murderer, but he must be silenced in a way that he has absolutely no credibility left when it's over. That way, even if he got lucky, nobody would believe him. I've got a backdoor connection to the *Chronicle* and our local channel. He will live, Chief, but only after a fashion." McGrady was about to renew his protest but Locke was gone.

Chapter Thirteen

Wo Chin bowed, pressing his palms together, holding the staff at the center of his chest. "I have passed through the eleven trials, and study now the 12th Circle Mastery of Zahu." It was spoken as he had been taught when confronted by an enemy: a warning. Listening to their continued laughter, even more uproarious than before, he somehow knew that he could not be the one speaking anymore, could not be standing there as a boy of eighteen, frail in the presence and smell of the hideous barbarians. Without words or thought, it came to him that his being was cleansed of fear.

The Friday night crowd from Union Street's upscale bars were streaming out at closing time as Jon Lee and Mike blended in, going towards Locke's San Francisco office just past Scott. It was one of the first restored Victorians complete with an ornate wrought iron fence, grass and flower beds and a brick path leading to the stairs and porch. It was almost too perfect. They turned up Scott and went around to the alley, through another wrought iron gate and into the shadows of the rear porch.

"There's probably no more than a five-minute window on his silent alarm," Jon Lee said as he *opened* the door. "That should give us about ten minutes' tops before the PD shows up."

"Now he tells me."

They hurried up the hall. "I imagine his office is upstairs."

There appeared to be identical copies of the portraits in the Oakland office, again hung behind a secretary's desk with double doors on opposite walls. They entered the one with the brass letters, "Charles Locke," that overlooked Union Street whose street light illuminated the room. They had flashlights and Mike carried a camera smaller than the palm of his hand. The oak flooring had no rug and groaned with every step they took as Mike began at the desk and Jon Lee peered into a wall of glass enclosed bookcases.

"Pretty impressive book collection," Jon Lee remarked. "Wonder who his decorator was. There was a banging sound from below and Mike turned from the desk to the high, wide, round window behind him.

"Couple of happy yuppie drunks careening off the iron fence."

"That must smart."

"Heading home for a little pick up romance? You see anything?"

Mike had checked the doors and scanned the leather couch, coffee and end tables to the right of the desk but there was nothing. "Coming up short." He was moving away from the desk when his foot hit something. "Hold on." He pulled the tan leather tube from under the desk."

"That's got to be the one from the other office."

"It's empty."

Jon Lee was opening the paneled doors on the bookcase.

"I'll go check the lobby." Mike's footsteps creaked across the floor and died on the reception carpet. There was nothing there and the door to Neilson's office on the other side was locked. As he hurried back to join Jon Lee, something strange caught the corner of his eye and he stopped. The wall on the right side of the door to Locke's office was at least ten feet to the back wall. Yet when you entered the office the wall of bookcases was only set about three feet back from that side of the door. "Hey, something's off here. We've got about a seven-foot play in this wall."

Jon Lee looked up. "And less than five minutes to get out of here. Let's start opening these glass panels. Look for buttons, pull the books out, anything. It's our last chance. Did you check the desk drawers, the panels under it?"

Mike nodded. "We Pulitzer guys are thorough." He opened the first panel of books and started pulling as Jon Lee began at the other end. Jon Lee was down to the bottom shelf in the second section when suddenly there was a creaking noise in the first section, and a snap. Flashing his light in there he saw the opening and pushed the entire shelf. It swung quietly inward and a light came on in a room behind the cases that ran the length of the wall behind the book shelves. There was an open armoire that held a row of what looked to be very expensive fur coats, and next to it was a small safe. Next to the outside wall stood a drafting table, with a series of drawings held down with small leather-encased weights. Mike closed the door so the light wouldn't reflect into the office." What have we got?"

Jon rifled through the plans. "I don't know. The one I saw is here. The rest look like the specs on that tunnel and hidden room, but look at these." Mike started to look, but noticed a rolled set leaning against the table and opened them quickly.

"Check this out. These must be the originals. Look at the dates and there's the sign-off by the city."

"And these with the tunnel don't have any dates. So, no approval. A pirate job."

"Right. Let me see what you were talking about." Mike pulled out his camera. "I'm going to photo all of them and the originals."

"We're out of time, man."

"I know. I can't understand these last few pages. It looks like the room interior but what's this funnel shaped thing in it and the grid above and below?"

"Just shoot it and let's go." They finished photographing the plans. "I hope you had film in that camera."

They shut the door in the bookcase, but it wouldn't click shut. "I just hope they come out." Mike glanced out the window. "Black and white across the street."

They reached the landing when the front door rattled, then footsteps going back down the front steps. "They've got to have somebody in the alley by now."

"No sweat, I relocked that door. Let's go." They heard the backdoor knob being turned as they slowly went out the front and tiptoed down the stairs, along the brick path and out onto Union. The bars had closed and there was almost no one on the street as they walked away.

The late winter dawn through the curtains would have been only a part of the dream McGrady was having. The girl from the chorus from last month's opera was running ahead of him from the ocean. Her naked body glistened and her long hair swung back and forth across her ass in a single long white-blonde braid. She was running toward a native hut with a palm thatched roof and a broad front deck. "Hurry," she turned slightly and called back, and he saw her high, firm breasts, "I want you so much!"

He was having trouble keeping up and he looked down and saw that his police uniform pants and underwear were soaked from the sea and hanging down on his ankles. As he looked back up, the deck was suddenly filled with small children from all over the world. A stern looking woman who reminded him of his third-grade teacher, Miss Wells, was ringing a school bell in her hand and the blonde was back in her opera costume. They were all, except Miss Wells, waving and laughing at him. She wouldn't stop ringing the bell and then something pushed his arm.

"Dan, it's the phone," his wife said next to him.

He didn't even try to open his eyes and fumbled around on the night table on his side of the bed. He got the receiver before the rest of the phone fell to the carpet with a partially filled glass of water. "Hello. McGrady."

"Go to another phone so your wife doesn't hear this conversation. Now!" It was Charles Locke and the chief had never heard his voice sound so high-pitched and crazy.

"Okay, I'm going." He got up, speaking in the dark to his wife. "Business. Go back to sleep, I'll take it in the den." He staggered down the hall, banging into the door as he reached the den, and grabbed the phone on the coffee table. "I'm back. What's the matter?"

"I've had another break-in, goddamn it! My office on Union Street."

"Holy shit. Is anything missing?"

"So far it doesn't look like it but they found my inner room where I keep personal valuables and other things, plans and such. Sometimes you can't be too careful when you're bidding a large project. Other developers have been known to break in."

"So, you think it might be that?"

"No! That's just it, nothing was missing."

"Okay, I'll come down as soon as I'm dressed."

"God!"

"Maybe it wasn't Koshima who broke into your other office."

"I told you, my men positively identified him."

"But why would he break into your other office?"

"That's what puzzles and worries me."

"Assuming it was him."

"Yes. But I have a hunch it was. We've got to stop him."

"Charles, our agreement was that I wasn't going to be a party to anything unlawful."

"I said, stop him. Don't do anything unlawful."

"But what could he know?" McGrady pushed his fingers back through his remaining hair.

"I don't know, goddamn it!"

"Let me...."

197

"I'm going to handle it." He hung up.

Chapter Fourteen

*"I am most impressed. See how I quake with
fear at the sight of you. You, what? A boy not half
grown? See how I tremble?" The warlord shook in
mock terror. Then, turning to his men, he asked if any
had heard of this powerful Zahu magic the monk had
spoken of. A voice shouted back that what he had heard
was only legend, but those who practiced this form of
combat were supposedly formidable opponents. "You
mean, when they are bigger than a mouse, hey?"
Again, his eyes riveted on the monk. "Is this true?"'
Wo Chin only bowed again in answer. "Then we shall
see." He called two of his men, smaller than the rest
but much larger than the monk. "Destroy this religious
worm so that we may continue our quest to his
monastery!"*

Dama gently pushed back the quilt and sat on
the edge of her bed. She was already dressed in a black
cashmere turtle neck and jeans. She eased her feet
slowly into a pair of soft, black leather boots. She
walked to the high narrow windows. There was a half-
moon covering the small park across the street and it
cut across the white rug to her dresser where she

199

quickly combed out her hair. She had not seen him for a week because the days she'd gone to the beach it had been well past his practice time. She'd called twice but there was no answer and she didn't dare leave her phone number on the message machine. She had to see him.

Out in the wide, high, long hallway off which were all the other rooms in the suite, she could hear nothing, except, perhaps, the television from Rasheed's room. But he would not check on her. Taking her shoulder bag and down parka from the entry closet, she turned the brass handle and the front door opened without a sound.

The front desk clerk was in the back office and she hurried across the red and grey marble and out the brass framed double front doors. It was almost 1:30 and the streets were empty except for an occasional car or taxi. She ran across and down California past the stately Pacific Union Club where she turned the corner at Mason and walked briskly downhill under the trees past the auto lobby and entrance to the Fairmont Hotel. Down the steep incline of Mason, Dama glanced over at the broad, high windows of the San Francisco Municipal Railroad cable car barn. The giant grey wheels that turned the cables were silent in the soft light from somewhere above and they reminded her of the wheels that opened and closed the locks on the Suez Canal.

To be sure, she had taken this walk a dozen times, so the store fronts and old buildings were familiar as she turned down Jackson, crossed Powell and went deeper into Chinatown to Grant where she turned left. The only activity on the street was some butchers in a shop on the corner cutting up ducks on a long table on the other side of the street.

She turned up the alley she'd discovered which led to Columbus. Although she was a little apprehensive, she wasn't frightened. But then she saw the three men standing outside the bar across the alley from the City Lights Book Store. She tried to divert her gaze but they saw her and one shouted out. "Hey, baby. How much for all night, huh? I wanta bury myself in that long-ass hair, baby."

Two of them started to follow her as he turned and walked past the brightly lit windows of the bookstore. "Hey, baby, wait....'sokay...no kiddin." When she reached the corner at Broadway she was frightened, but just as the men had almost reached her a policeman emerged from the shadows of a doorway.

"Are you okay, miss?"

"Yes, thank you, officer. I was going home. I live up on Telegraph Hill and those men started following me from that bar back there."

He glared at the two semi-drunks and walked towards them. "Get your butts back in the bar. You can't even tell a lady when you see one." They turned quickly and disappeared.

"Which way is home."

"The steps at Montgomery."

"I'll walk you that far."

"Thank you."

They crossed Broadway and then Columbus and walking on the side where the *Thigh and ?* Club was located. "You sound English."

"I was educated there. My home is in the desert, not far from Mecca."

"Well, it's probably a lot safer there than here." They'd reached the bottom of the long steep stairs.

"I can make it now. I'm not far from the top of the stairs."

"Okay. But I'll wait until you're out of sight."

"Thank you, officer. You are very kind." He tipped his hat, and when she reached the top she turned and waved down at him and disappeared into the dark cover of the trees. She knew the way exactly but began to hesitate the closer she came. Would he be upset? It was very late. She tiptoed down the path to his door and smelled the rich aroma of the pine and cedar bonsai on his front porch. Her knock was as delicate as a bird. She waited. She thought she heard something and knocked just as softly again.

The door opened so smoothly it seemed like magic and he was standing there in a blue kimono with a wide yellow sash.

"Dama, my God. What are you doing here?" He put his arm around her and escorted her inside and down the hall. The light in the living room which looked out on the deck came from the moon and the white glowing embers of an earlier fire in the open river stone hearth. He took her coat and gloves and held her cold hands in his. "Your hands are freezing. Here, come sit by the fire." She sunk into the deep cushions and he put three logs on the fire. They began to flame almost instantly. "I'll be right back."

He went behind the granite counter with three stools that separated the kitchen and living room and found a hot water bottle in a lower cupboard which he filled with hot water and brought to her. "Put this on your knees and your hands on top. They'll be warm soon. My mother used to do that when my dad, brother and I'd come home from a cold day's fishing at the wharf." He smiled. "It always works. Oh, something else." He went into the bedroom and returned with a clean pair of white wool socks. "Let me." He kneeled in front of her and gently pulled off the boots and put on the socks. As he was doing this, Dama reached out timidly but without hesitation and touched his forehead, running her long fingers across his right temple and down until it stopped on his cheek.

He looked up at her as their faces were embraced by the firelight and his hand met hers. Slowly, he leaned forward and his sigh met hers as they kissed fully, unselfconsciously, as if they had all the time in the world, as if it would go on forever.

"Thank you," he said quietly. "Thank you." They kissed again and she leaned back on the cushions, pulling him towards her until his face lay against her breasts and she closed his eyes, running her hands through his hair as his hands caressed her back and waist. They remained like that until he raised his head and smiled. "My legs are getting stiff." She giggled. "How about a glass of red wine?" She nodded.

He rose from his knees, but she wouldn't let go of his arms and he leaned forward again with his arms resting on the couch and kissed her forehead and cheek. As he stood, he pulled her up with him and they held each other, letting their cheeks, noses, lips and chins move slowly over each other like a blind person might feel a new face for the first time. They walked arm in arm past the granite topped island with three high chairs that separated the living room from his kitchen. He opened a bottle of Merlot and poured them each a glass. He handed her a glass and she pressed close to him as they toasted, kissed and returned to the couch where they watched the bouncing flames on the hearth and across the hardwood floor.

"Please, promise me. You will never again come alone at night."

She sighed. "After tonight I may not be able to ever come again." Her delicate fingers weaved patterns on his left hand which she had taken and placed in her lap.

"Don't say that Dama, please. Now that you're here, you just can't leave."

"There will be hell to pay from my guardians tomorrow."

"You mean those guys at the beach?"

"No, they are just part of the security that came with us. It is Rasheed. He is here, as am I, on my father's business." She paused, leaned over and kissed Jon Lee again. "He wants me to marry him. My father saved him from the streets of Mecca when he was a child. Actually, it was my brother Abyase who did, but father raised Rasheed with us like a son. I sometimes think his allegiance to my father is stronger than my brother's."

Jon Lee laid his head on her shoulder. "Wow, that was a lot to take in at once. You say it straight, I'll never have to worry about you speaking up."

She lifted her head and covered his with her hair. "My old tutor, Burta, always told me all marriage was communications."

"He must be a very wise man," he said in a muffled tone.

205

"What was that? I didn't hear you."

"I'm lost in a dark forest and it's hard to speak or see or even breathe, but I love it." She lifted her head and threw her hair back over the couch. "Ah, light." He turned to her. "And incredible beauty." He ran a finger from her chin to the top of her cheekbone. "What about Rasheed and what business of your father are you doing here?"

She sat up and leaned against the arm of the couch. Her head and hair were backlit by the fire. "I won't marry Rasheed and my father knows that. I'm sorry, Jon Lee, I can't really speak of his business. Please don't question me. I have only another month here. I want to spend as much of it with you as I dare. We return home to Mecca and the desert in about three or four weeks, depending on whether all the business is complete. Just trust me. His business is ultimately world peace. And I believe he can achieve it."

"My master has always said that when the question is posed in silence the answer soon arrives."

"What does that mean? And who is this master?"

"It means you can't answer a question until it's ready to be answered. So, don't ask it. And my master comes from an ancient line of monks who practiced what you've seen me do at the beach, Zahu. I'm also a teacher but this part of my training does not allow me to talk with my master and he's like a second father, in many ways more than that. It has been hard." He held up the wine glass and through it he could see the first dawn out of the east beginning a grey and purple light across his deck. "I've been drinking way too much of this, only worse, whiskey."

"My father says alcohol is only bad when we become its slave, but he personally holds to the old ways which means no alcohol."

"Well, I don't think I'm quite a slave to it yet. I just find my work so depressing." He leaned over and they kissed long again, and turned to watch the increasing light in the east.

"You should see the sun rise and set in the Sahara once before you die."

"Will you take me?" She smiled sadly. "You have to have one real American breakfast before you die, although it might kill you." He joked as she looked with deep affection at him.

"I must get back. But I would like that."

They climbed down the rickety old stairs on the bay side of Telegraph Hill, traversed the gnarl of railroad tracks and walked with arms around each other along the piers until they reached the tiny wooden cabin-like building that was the Eagle Café where the longshoremen ate their breakfast. Jon Lee ordered her the works, complete with a slice of thick, crisp bacon, one sausage, a small piece of ham, an egg, hash browns and toast with some processed orange juice thrown in. He had the same.

The place was still fairly empty at 5:15 and they ate in silence, sometimes looking long at each other, and watched the counter stools and wooden tables begin to fill up. By the time they'd finished, there was no place to sit.

Back outside, there was a crystal sky and the shadow of Telegraph Hill was growing ever smaller as the sun rose higher. He showed her Fisherman's Wharf and Aquatic Park. They rode a cable car up Hyde, getting off at Washington and Mason, just below Nob Hill and next to the cable car barn she'd passed earlier. They walked up very slowly into the trees and stopped at the edge of the small park. She glanced up at the top floor of the Huntington Hotel and he led her behind a series of trees where no one could see them.

"I hope you aren't in too much trouble."

"I'll handle it. I'm not a good liar but hopefully Rasheed will believe me. I went for a walk at 5:00, rode the first cable car to the wharf, had breakfast and returned." She put his arms around her waist and placed her forehead against his lips.

"When can we meet again?" He kissed her.

She drew back and looked up at him. Her stare was unflinching as she spoke. "I can't promise, Jon Lee, though in this moment I want you to take me away

208

from here until they give up looking for me and go
home. I want that so much, more than anything."

"Oh God, I do too, Dama."

"But I have responsibilities to my father which I
can't forsake, please try to understand. And please
don't try to contact me. It might be dangerous for you.
Jon Lee, we may meet again tomorrow. Yet, maybe
never again." Tears began to run down both of their
cheeks and they embraced.

"My master has gone and now you, the first
woman I've ever understood love with." He hit his
palm with the bamboo staff. "Just like that, gone."
They embraced until she forced herself to let go.

"I'm sorry, Jon Lee. I feel that love too. I'll try.
Please trust me." She turned abruptly and hurried
across the park through the wet grass.

The lobby was completely empty as she walked
to the elevator. The clock by the front desk said 6:50.
She hoped she could get to her room undetected, but
when she opened the door Rasheed was standing with
his back to her half way down the wide hall in an
oatmeal robe, and whirled around as she entered.

"Where have you been?!"

"I woke up early and couldn't sleep so I decided
to take an early morning walk and ended up riding to
the wharf, having breakfast and now I'm back. I was
fine. This is not a dangerous city."

"You have no basis to say that, Dama." He touched her forearms in the thick, puffy down parka as if she'd just been discovered after a long absence. "Please, never wander in a city of heathens like this. You could have been hurt, abducted, anything. Please." She felt deep sympathy for his urgent look and kissed both his cheeks.

"I'm very sorry, Rasheed. Please forgive me."

He looked at the high ceiling and then at her. "I am charged by your father to protect you with my life."

"I know. It was foolish. Please, forgive me."

His face softened a little. "I forgive you if you promise never to do such a foolish thing." She nodded and he sighed deeply. "All right."

"Thank you, Rasheed. I know how much you care. Now, I must go and see how Designate 8 is doing this morning so we can report to father at eleven."

"I forgot to tell you last night. Your brother arrives with the team from the laboratory in a couple of days to complete the most important part of the construction project. Things move ahead of schedule, the developer informs us. So, finally we may return home."

"I will be happy to see Abyase." Dama smiled, but as she turned to walk to her room her face seemed to fall. How would she ever see Jon Lee again with her brother coming so soon?

The next morning, Jon Lee had just made some tea and was waiting for an English muffin to pop out of his toaster. He turned on the tiny TV on the kitchen counter, the only one in the house. He muted the religious show that came on just before the morning news and went in to make his bed and straighten up the bedroom which never needed much straightening since he was so neat. The whole house had a defining Japanese look, uncluttered but with a few pictures and ceramic pieces which he'd obviously taken a long time to choose and an even longer time to find the exact right place for. He heard the toaster pop and went back to the kitchen. It was a particularly warm day for early May and he could feel the heat through the deck French doors as he crossed the living room.

A commercial was just ending and he unmuted the sound as the smiling faces of the local morning anchors appeared. His day had begun, as his days off usually did, at 5 with a long barefoot run on Ocean Beach followed by a walking meditation as the tide lapped his feet. He and Mike were meeting with the District Attorney, Carney Landsberger at eleven to discuss what they'd learned and, hopefully, receive some off-the-record guidance.

He spread some fresh ground peanut butter on his muffin and sipped coffee as the news began. The male news anchor had once covered the crime beat for the station so Jon Lee knew him. In his new role, he seemed even more shallow and vacuous.

"Good morning. Our top story today concerns the strange death of a patient at County Hospital. We go now to Jill Meyers at the hospital. Jill, what can you tell us?"

"Good morning, Harry." The reporter was standing on the edge of a pathway in one of the small gardens that surrounded the hospital and the area directly in front of her—a yellow and purple ground cover—was cordoned off by yellow police tape.

"Sometime between eleven last night and five this morning, a patient here plunged to his death from the fifth floor, even though we understand he was being held on the sixth floor in the security section of the hospital. He was thirty-seven-year-old Joseph Anfuso, the alleged hitman in the death of seven-year-old Natasha Dobkovnic some months ago. Anfuso had been in and out of a coma and was being guarded by…."

Jon Lee turned off the television and shouted, "shit!" He went out into the fresh morning air and began to breathe slowly to calm the anger running through his entire body. Without information from him, things would just unravel more. He went back in the kitchen and pulled a bottle of Jack Daniels from under the sink and practically tore off the sealed label and top. He stood looking at it for a moment and then lifted it to his lips, filling his mouth. He paused, feeling it begin to trickle down his throat. Then he leaned over and forcefully spat it out.

At 10:45, he met Mike in the lobby of the flamboyant district attorney's office. "You heard the news?" Mike asked. Jon Lee nodded. "That guy had a leg amputated. There's no way he could have come out of a coma, unplugged himself, gotten to a fifth-floor window without the SID seeing him, and then, throw himself down into a flower bed."

"I don't know why whoever put this out just didn't waste him months ago?"

"Maybe they figured he wouldn't wake up from one of the comas and it would save them the trouble."

"Or they were worried about something that was about to unfold."

The DA's secretary came for them and they walked down a long hall with the sterile look of so many government offices to a plain dark wood door at the end. Inside, Carney was sitting at his desk, feet up, looking out the window towards the Embarcadero. Though dressed in a rumpled grey three-piece suit with

an open collar and his tie loosened, he always wore
Bierkenstock sandals. He claimed it was for medical
reasons but Mike had a hunch it was just another of
Carney's ways of thumbing his nose at the system, and
getting away with it because he was so good at his job.
If you crossed him or tried to play money and politics
with him, your life got miserable fast. He possessed a
quality the voters could see but was seldom found in
public servants; Carney had integrity and nobody was
about to buy it from him.

He was a short, stocky man, bald, with bits of
curly uncombed hair half covering his ears. Nose, eyes,
lips and ears: everything was big about his round pale
face. "It's Mr. P and the boychik with the stick.
Welcome to my humble kingdom." They shook hands
and he motioned them to a grey flannel covered couch
on the far wall as he fell back into a seat across the
coffee table from them. "So, what's shakin', brothers?"

"You saw the hospital story this morning?"

He pointed to his desk which was piled a foot
high with briefs and a plaque with his name in
conservative sized letters with smaller print under it that
said, *One Mean Mother*. "It's in my daily briefing but I
haven't read it. Stopped watching TV years ago. Bad
for the psyche. What's happened?"

"The hitman went out the window at County."

Carney sat up and put his short arms on the arm rests. "Come on." He looked at both of them. "No joke?"

"We wish," Jon Lee replied.

"You wish?" Carney hit the bald spot with his palm, raising his eyebrows and shaking his head at the same time. "I thought McGrady was handling this personally with the SID? What have we here, former cop and a wacko with a stick doing their own investigation?" They smiled at him and shrugged as if they were innocent. "You guys, I don't know. You shouldn't be talking to the DA. I can see lots of illegal potential here."

He paused. "So, I'm dreaming the conversation about to take place, right? When I wake up I won't remember a thing?"

"Agreed." Mike couldn't help but smile.

"And?"

"Dreaming, naturally. We've been poking around and the questions are interesting. Why the SID presence in the Malloy? Why the harassment of three residents whose property Charles Locke now owns?"

"Correction, he owns the other one now too." Mike and Jon Lee looked at each other in surprise and then back at Carney. "Not as dumb as I look, huh? Stay tuned. Continue."

"Okay, make that four. Why would Locke hire a hitman to take out the Russian when he could have used velvet gloves just as effectively? Given the SID presence, is there any connection between Locke and McGrady?"

Carney stretched. "Good questions, lads. Let me throw in another one. How can McGrady afford to put a down payment on a two-hundred-acre vineyard up in St. Helena?"

"What?"

"Look, friends. My sources told me from the get-go that this mob-drug connection was bogus. And look what's happened? Since that Corfu, whatever, project is going up a mile a minute, where's the SID gone? Yes, I've been on this for some time too. Oh, and why would a guy with his finger in every deal in town offer those people twice the market value for their homes? I think there's a lot that fits here but I don't know where to put the pieces. Let's say McGrady is getting a pay off by Locke to use the SID. Why? He could have built that project a dozen other places with no strain. Why right there?"

"Across the street from my mother's."

"And my home now."

Carney wiggled his toes through his socks and relaxed back into the chair. He studied their faces for a moment. "Come on, you guys aren't telling me something."

They looked at each other and laughed. "Great instincts, Carney."

"No better than yours when you were a cop, Mr. Pulitzer. Come on, what?"

"Well…dreaming, of course, Jon Lee made a little visit to Locke's Oakland office and…"

"Boychik, you are bad. That's how his people got their ouchies." He pointed his finger at Jon Lee who acknowledged this.

"And I came up empty, except the positive connection with Locke and the hitman, who is probably down in dark waters with the bottom feeders, dropped off by Locke's yacht most likely. The Wind, something or other."

"*Windhover*," Carney interrupted. "Remember your English poetry? Gerard Manley Hopkins."

"How'd you know that?"

"Let's just say I've been looking into some of Locke's deals too."

"But there's just a little more."

"I was afraid of that."

"We…."

"As in together?" Carney asked.

"We made a visit to Locke's Union Street office about a week ago."

"You guys weren't very tidy either."

"There's a hidden room we got into and found plans for that Corfu project. There was an original set, dated and signed off, and another set involving what looks like a room into the hillside from the underground garage that obviously hadn't been approved."

"Connection?"

"We're dry."

Carney snapped his fingers and got up. "Let's mosey over to County. I've got a hunch, based upon some info I got recently."

They drove to County Hospital and parked a block away. Carney got out. "I'm going to go up and see what the autopsy looks like. Sit tight."

He was back in less than ten minutes. "What I figured."

"Drugs?" Jon Lee asked.

"Right, boychik. Hallucinatory in nature. Specifically, many, many milligrams of LSD. Conclusion, he got his brain fried."

"Sounds like a cover to me. There's no way he could have gone out of a window. Logic tells us he got *escorted* to a window without bars."

"Definitely." Carney got into the driver's seat. "Oh, another thing. The name of Locke's yacht, *Windhover*." He looked at them. "Think. I read your report. You heard that dead guy's words, Jon Lee. Remember? Something like *bird*? Windhover. Bird."

Jon Lee laughed. "Got it. That just reinforces the connection, but that guy's testimony would have been more powerful."

"Agreed, but how many courts you think would convict one of the most powerful business leaders and donors to so many local charitable causes on the conclusion that now he's shooting people to buy property for twice what it's worth. There's a hell of a lot more going on here that we don't know. That's the DA's gut feeling." He stared out the window, thinking. "Mike, what about those other plans, going into the hill?"

"Don't know. There was one drawing showing a kind of cylinder with a grid pattern suspended above and below it. It could just be some new kind of heating or air conditioning unit."

Carney tapped out a rhythm on the steering wheel, then turned to look at them. "Mike, what about this nut scientist you know? I vaguely remember he helped us on a case maybe fifteen years ago. Is he still around?"

"Good thought, Carney. I'll give him a call. It can't hurt.

Designate 8 left his office at one, telling his secretary he was going to do some shopping after lunch and would return around three or four. He put on a velvet dark green Borsolino hat and his sunglasses when he didn't want to be seen or recognized, and rode the California cable car to the last stop at Market. The Sausalito ferry was just ready to pull away and he hurried on board and went up to the top deck where he got some coffee and went outside to stand by the railing as the ferry headed into the bay.

      The ride across always had a calming effect on him and, besides Mt. Noe, this was always where he came to think and reflect. He looked towards the hills of Marin County and thought about Martha. He'd been up to visit her the previous weekend and though he knew her nodding and smiling didn't mean she understood anymore, it did him good just to share his concerns. He'd told her about the United Nations *Week of Peace* which was coming up soon and about Esse.

      "He's a good man, Martha. Wants us to live in peace. Just like you were always working for. And he has the power behind him to make it happen." He'd taken her hand then and noticed how thin and frail it looked. "It's, well, I just keep having these nagging doubts as to whether I'm doing the right thing in helping him." He looked into her eyes but they were blue and empty. "He got so angry once. It has just stuck with me." She smiled and patted his hand. "I'm probably just being silly."

      The ferry horn startled him and he realized that they were about to dock in Sausalito. He scanned the dock. His old friend was standing there. They had lunch once a month lunch since his friend had moved over to

Sausalito and bought a little cottage up on the hill above the town. He said he loved it and Designate 8 was happy for him. Homer Thween and he had known each other since first grade. For fifty-plus years now he'd been a dependable and faithful friend.

As he was going down the stairs, Martha's soft face came to him. Had she been trying to tell him something about Esse and his world vision?

Chapter Fifteen

The two smiled in anticipation and raised their swords. The blades glinted blood red and silver in the dying sun. They came forward and slowly began to circle Wo Chin. Without thinking, he did what always before, even after many hours of practice, had been awkward; he assumed the 'open defense' posture of the 12th Circle. But now his arms and legs, his whole body seemed to flow easily into it, his staff held lightly in his right hand as he followed the movements of the two barbarians. At that instant, he was overcome by the feeling of being suddenly invisible. Then they struck as one, their swords flashing down upon Wo Chin's body. What happened next caused even the warlord to step back.

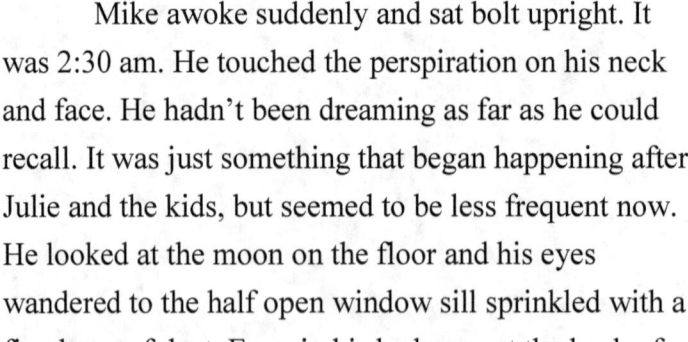

Mike awoke suddenly and sat bolt upright. It was 2:30 am. He touched the perspiration on his neck and face. He hadn't been dreaming as far as he could recall. It was just something that began happening after Julie and the kids, but seemed to be less frequent now. He looked at the moon on the floor and his eyes wandered to the half open window sill sprinkled with a fine layer of dust. Even in his bedroom at the back of the house, the residue from the construction project was everywhere. Billy and Ellen had finally sold and moved down the hill. Luckily, the heavy work had been completed, and they were working mostly inside now except for a strange crew that arrived early each day in two limousines. They all looked foreign and worked inside the garage, leaving for lunch at exactly noon and returning at two each day. He was walking down to catch the bus to work and happened to see the foreman who he asked about the limo crew. He just shook his head and volunteered that he thought they were pretty weird, but they were specialists installing some new ecologically sound heating and air-conditioning system in a room in the garage. In fact, he'd had to divert one of his crews to other work until that was finished because he was told the garage was off limits until then. Mike rolled over and had almost drifted back into sleep when the phone rang.

"Hello." A drunken voice away from the phone was singing what sounded like a Japanese lullaby. "Hello?"

"Yo, Pop…is me…. former partner in justice…. or whatever."

"Where are you, former partner?"

"Second…rah…ring of the Inferno. You know the place. Chinatown. Little celebration of justice going on and I guess I'm the only one celebrating."

223

"Don't do this, Jon Lee. We got Carney on our side now."

"Yeah but hitman dead. No testimony. Locke, real big man. Justice gonna be crushed again, Pop." He seemed to be laughing at what he'd just said.

"Easy. We've still got a way to go before you can say that."

"Always ends up so. They kill. You put 'em in. They out. Shit."

"Where are you? Give me a street and wait right there. I can be down in twenty minutes."

"Nah, sssss…is okay. Go home with bonsai. Sleep."

"Get a taxi, don't try to drive." The phone went to dial tone.

Jon Lee dropped the phone and it swung on its cord, banging against the phone booth a couple of times and hung silent again. He could see his Porsche a half a block away but kept leaning against the booth, mumbling Yee Chin's name over and over like a mantra. "Yee Chin…Chin…Yee…"

Suddenly he bought the staff up directly in front of his neck and rolled across the cement behind a trash can. He looked at the dart stuck into it, pulled it out, smelled its tip and threw it into the can. Somebody was out there but he didn't care. "Who cares? Lady with the blindfold and scale? Who?" He rose slowly and listened but he could detect neither sound nor movement. The staff rose again, but his instincts had been blunted enough that this time the dart, coming from behind him, struck his shoulder and held. He struggled to pull it out and it fell into the gutter in a circle of lamp light. He tried to hurry towards his car but the harder he tried, the slower he seemed to move until he was down on his knees. He reached the Porsche's front fender, fell against it and passed out.

Out of the darkness, three men approached from different directions. The largest one cautiously touched Jon Lee's shoulder. "He's definitely out."

The other two came up next to him and they looked down at Jon Lee. "Man, I'm glad we didn't have to meet him sober. Could you believe his instincts, even as drunk as he is?"

The light had just begun to turn into dawn when he heard Anna's frantic voice calling up to him. He hurried to open the door. She was standing in the entry barefoot in her robe. "Oh, Mike. You drive me please?"

"What is it?"

"Naga just call. Jon Lee in hospital. Please, you drive me."

In less than forty-five minutes, they were waiting in the emergency room with a dozen other people. It smelled like somebody had mixed urine, blood, alcohol and sweat together and let it dry in the sun. The clock said 6:20 by the reception desk. Naga came out and hugged his mother who'd been crying. He was a head shorter than Jon Lee but had similar hair, except his was very short, making him look more like a monk than a doctor.

"He's okay, Momma." He looked at Mike. "Yes, he'd been drinking. Double blood alcohol. The Porsche banged into four or five parked cars. PD bought him in. Strange, his captain got here so quick. He just left. Jon Lee is suspended pending a departmental investigation. It's only a traffic matter, a DUI, but he is a lieutenant with the PD. That changes things. He says he never got into the car, which means somebody gave him a friendly assist when he was out. There's probably not a soul in this city besides Yee Chin who could subdue him sober. He was hit by a dart in the right shoulder. If I had it, maybe I could extract something from its tip."

They looked up and Jon Lee was coming down the hall. His mother ran to him. "No worry now. All will be okay."

He kissed her. "You probably said that on the way to the internment camp." He hugged her.

"We go now, Naga?" She asked.

"Sure, Momma."

"Jon Lee."

He shook Mike's hand. "Thanks. Guess I really screwed up this time."

"They can't suspend you indefinitely for a DUI."

"But I wasn't…."

"Where were you when it happened?"

"Outside that bar up from Grant and Jackson. A dump. Hawaiian theme."

"Do you remember what happened to the dart?"

"I pulled it out and dropped in near a trash can."

"Naga, can you take them home?" Naga nodded.

"I'm going to have a look. Unless your friends picked it up, given the way the streets are swept, it might still be there."

"I'll be up in the psyche ward on three when I get back if you find it." Naga took his mother's arm and Jon Lee the other and they started toward the exit.

Mike knew the bar and started walking the gutter. He found the dart wedged under some leaves and a discarded plastic diaper. He put his handkerchief around it, and was up at Jon Lee's as Naga was just coming up the path. "That was fast." Mike handed him the handkerchief. "I can't promise anything."

"How's your mom?" Naga shook his head to indicate she'd survive. "How about him?"

"We just need to give him space I think. He's the only person I know that can meditate and get answers. He'll figure things out. I imagine he'll be back to work in a week."

He would let Jon Lee call him. Mike decided to lay back himself. But after a couple days, curiosity got the best of him and after it was dark and the crews were gone he walked across and up into the underground garage. It was completely dark, but the full moon gave him enough light to find the door in the back wall. It had a black and yellow sign on it marked "Dangerous. Do not Enter." He tried the handle anyway and it was locked. He was standing there engrossed in thought when someone touched his shoulder and he nearly jumped. It was Teri. A student who had an all glass studio on the roof of a building three doors up from Billy had moved and Teri had rented it.

"My, aren't we jumpy." She kissed his cheek. "I really didn't mean to startle you. I was just coming around the corner when I saw you come here."

"That's okay. It hasn't been a good week. My friend Jon Lee was suspended."

"I know. I talked to Anna for a long time yesterday. I hope someday, if the Gods favor it, that I can be as concerned a mom as she is. She's really worried. It's been a week and they haven't reinstated him yet."

"I know."

"What are you looking for here, one of those Arabs?"

"I don't know, I really don't. Come on, you look like you could use that nightcap tonight."

"I could, but you're not ready yet."

"How do you know? When will I be?"

"It's the way you ask. But I can wait. I'm not going anywhere, unless they decide to build another one of these Corfu monstrosities." They said good night and he watched her walk up the street carrying her workout bag over one shoulder, the long grayish blonde hair combed down her back.

He sat for a long time, sharing the moonlit darkness with the ferns which seemed to gather around him in solace. He missed the lights from Thween's and the Dobkovnic's. Now there were just the layers of cement like giant steps pushed into the hillside. When the phone rang, he didn't feel like picking it up but thought it might be Jon Lee.

"Hello."

"Naga, Mike. Did I wake you?"

"No, just sitting here."

"I found what I needed to from that dart but I'm afraid it's too strange to do Jon Lee much good."

"What do you mean?" Mike turned on the lamp next to the phone.

"I had a friend run at least a dozen tests. He's the best there is, Harvard, Mass. General, if anyone could find an answer he could. But we're ending up just with speculation, because the substance on that dart is something he's never examined before. And, to his knowledge, neither has anyone else. It's beyond our research right now. All he could determine was that it was a completely organic compound, nothing synthetic. He said, and remember this is just a wild guess, that in looking at the molecular structure he thinks it might act in the blood stream like a fireworks rocket. You know, it explodes, rushes to the brain, and then just falls away in sparks and vanishes in the night. That's how he thinks this affected Jon Lee. It went straight to his brain—bang!—and then just disappeared in the blood stream. Which leaves alcohol as the only evidence. And I'm sure that his Captain doesn't believe Jon Lee was lifted into his car, the engine started and put into gear….and we know the rest."

"Did you tell him?"

"And Momma too."

"You know what this means?"

"Yes. And so does he."

"How's he seem to you?"

"He actually sounded much better than I thought he would."

Surprisingly, Jon Lee welcomed the time off. He'd been suspended with pay so for now he didn't need to look for another job. It gave him more time for his practice both in meditation and at the dunes. Dama no longer came, though he would look down the beach at the end of every practice, hoping. He even walked the old neighborhoods that he and Mike had patrolled by car and on foot, sometimes running into an individual who recognized him and extended their sympathies since there'd been a story about the incident in the "City" section of the *Chronicle*.

But all during this time, he walked with the image of Dama's beauty in his mind's eye. Again, he was not drinking and would sit wrapped in a quilt for hours into the evening with hot tea as the approaching summer sky extended itself into longer evenings. One night he arrived home around midnight. He and Mike had heard nothing from Carney. and Andre was in Europe so they couldn't yet take the photos to him. As he lay down in the hammock on his deck, he detected the slightest movement below him, but he sensed that it was heavier than a small animal. There was certainly nothing left for the people in Chinatown to come after him again.

He slid softly out of the hammock and soundlessly moved to the edge of the deck. With one smooth motion, he sprung over the railing. He landed in the plants and brush facing under the deck in the *open defense* posture of the 12th Circle. "Identify yourself." He took a step under the deck and froze. Dama was cowering, kneeling between two large bushes.

231

"Jon Lee." Her voice was so small as he took her in his arms.

Chapter Sixteen

Instead of the heavy swords severing both the monk's arms, a terrifying cry of agony resounded over the plateau as the two barbarians fell to the ground, their necks partially severed and gushing blood. Their swords had found not the monk but each other, and Wo Chin stood now to one side in the same position of defense while the bodies twitched and wiggled until they rattled into death. Only the wind sounded in the clearing until Wo Chin spoke. "I am bound never to take life, only to defend it."

June overcast and wind had arrived in early May. Dama returned to the hotel one afternoon after an extended walk on Ocean Beach that had taken her all the way south to the zoo and back. The brisk weather mixing with the warmth of the fire going in the living room had made her drowsy. Although it was only mid-afternoon, the late spring light had begun to fade as it came quietly through the high windows and she took off her boots and stretched out on the high-backed sofa that faced the fire. She'd been on the verge of sleep when the front door opened and closed and footsteps came down the hall. Abyase and Rasheed had returned from the construction, and it sounded as if her brother was making an important point as they entered the living room.

"Now, my brother, is the time." They went and stood by the windows looking out at Grace Cathedral. "There can be no more delays. You must make your decision. The crystals will arrive at midnight by small plane at the San Jose private airport. We will pick them up and tomorrow the installation will be complete. By noon, Panjali will have run his tests."

"And, at last, we can go home?"

"The crew leaves tomorrow night with me, but your task remains unfinished. You and Dama return the end of the week. We must keep monitoring Designate 8 until this United Nations stupidity is over. We have no further use for him then."

Dama had lain still, staring at the floral designs painted on the high ceiling. What did Abyase want from Rasheed?

"But I must know your decision, Rasheed. Time grows short."

When Rasheed spoke after a long silence, his voice was strained. "What you ask of me, brother, is to betray the man who took me from the streets and raised me as his son."

"I am aware of the gravity of the decision, Rasheed, but his way will only perpetuate more of the same."

"But we have all this advanced power, Abyase. To be able to reduce this city to buildings alone, or to just people, or to nothing at all…. There could be no greater power."

"Yes, if he would use it. But he won't. Even with all the anger he has deep within him about his hand, about my dead older brother and the death of our mother, our father would never take human life. He saves little bugs even, you know that! When we found birds couldn't live in the holy city because of the air, we had to set free thousands when they could just have easily been killed. When I was six or seven, before you came to us, he took Dama and me out the secret entrance to the city into the desert for a picnic one day. Our people had just finished planting more palms next to those already in place by the pond to make a wind break if it was ever needed. The new trees were tiny and while he and Dama were getting out the meal, I ran in and out between them. Towards the far side, there was one that looked rather sickly and as I went around it I reached out and grabbed it and swung round. To my surprise, it came out of the sand.

"I have never seen him so angry. His face was red and he gave me a spanking that left me sore for two days. All he said was, 'The natural world is a gift to us, Abyase, and to abuse it is to abuse ourselves.' Don't you see, that's why he would never unleash all of Panjali's power."

From what had now become her hiding place, Dama had heard her brother's footsteps pacing back and forth as he spoke. "I have tried to live in his way, tried to see the logic of trying to bring about peace by showing the world what the worst version of the opposite could be….but I know it won't work. Why did I study history at Oxford? I knew it would either prove or disprove my father's vision. And time and again, the fools of this world have disproved it, as if they are incapable of learning history's lessons. Oh, the commoners, yes, they would follow my father in a moment. But those who hold the power never will, because their hedonism and greed for more power, more of their stupid money, will never allow them to change. So, the only way to world peace is to take their power away by showing them one so far advanced that it scares them to death and they cease their destructive ways under threat of annihilation."

"But you would use Panjali's power, this power that by tomorrow afternoon will be capable of being unleashed from that little room beneath the mountain?"

"And I will not hesitate to use it if my wishes are not met."

Dama had tried to fight back her tears but they were running freely down her cheeks now. Her own brother!

"But you would then kill not only the powerful but the innocent as well!"

"That would be the price at first. But I do not think they would be willing to see another major city and its people turned to rubble. You must make your choice, Rasheed. I have many followers in the Holy City who as we speak are capable of taking control immediately. If you are not for us, then we go different paths."

Rasheed had hit his palms against the window panes and rubbed his beard. "All right, I will confess. No one has been more loyal to our father than me. But I too have harbored and hidden those same thoughts for many years. I've tried to rid myself of them but they always return. The infidels must be crushed, if that is the way to keep them from destroying each other and this planet." He stared for a long moment at his brother. "I cannot help myself, Abyase."

Abyase reached out and they embraced. "I am stronger with your help, Rasheed. Come, we need to go over the final installation plans with the crew."

Their footsteps echoed down the high hallway. The front door had opened and closed and Dama was left alone. She'd sat up on the sofa and cried unrestrained. They would betray their own father. They would set loose the same violence on the world that they had pledged to prevent. Then she realized that she was all alone, except for Jon Lee. They would leave for the airport by 10:30. Then she would go to Jon Lee.

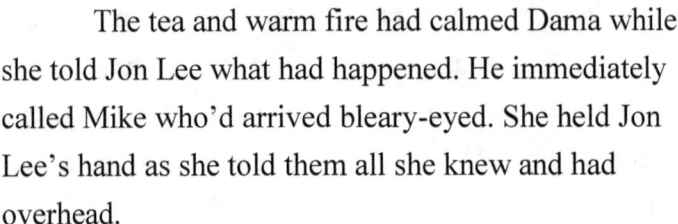

The tea and warm fire had calmed Dama while she told Jon Lee what had happened. He immediately called Mike who'd arrived bleary-eyed. She held Jon Lee's hand as she told them all she knew and had overhead.

"Panjali is like my uncle. As I was growing up, he would always bring me to the laboratories to show me what he called his *magic*. I don't know any details, but he showed me how he was going to, as he said, *borrow* a Russian satellite to transmit father's real time image to the United Nations celebration here soon."

"Less than ten days," Mike added.

"When he showed me the drawings, there was another object that also looked like a satellite but he just joked with me about that except to say it was American."

Jon Lee looked at Mike. "That's got to have some connection with this and what Andre picked up." Mike nodded.

"They are right now at a small airport in San Jose picking up some sort of crystals which the crew installs and tests tomorrow. Then the door will be sealed and they return home." She squeezed Jon Lee's hand. "I go with Rasheed by the end of the week. Rasheed and Abyase always had the plans on a drafting table in the den but I couldn't make much out of them."

She leaned back against his shoulder. "I don't know what to do."

"You aren't alone in this anymore, my love."

Less than two hours later they were driving through the gates of Andre's estate. He was standing by the massive front door encircled in fieldstone and was wearing a yellow nightshirt covered with Disney characters. "Welcome, pilgrims."

He'd made both coffee and tea, and as they sipped these at his kitchen table they laid out everything they knew for him. Andre listened and said nothing until they were finished. "The odds are better than fifty-fifty that those satellite beams are the ones coming down here. That answers the question of why they were disappearing into thin air. Neither has a connecting point. If those crystals are functional by tomorrow afternoon, then perhaps I can then trace their trajectory. Bingo. Come with me."

He led them down one wood paneled hall after another until they entered his laboratory which looked like a science fiction movie set. There, he spread out the pictures Mike had taken of the plans, grunting and talking to himself as if he'd forgotten their presence. Finally, he turned to them. "Very, very interesting. Let me show you something. They walked to the end of the lab and he pressed a key pad on the door. The room they entered was windowless and small. "This is where I keep the real spooky stuff I'm fooling with." At one side of the room there was something about five feet high under a tarp which Andre pulled away and let fall to the floor.

Dama gasped. "That is just like the drawing on the plans."

"Yes." Andre smiled. "And I would love to meet this chief scientist of your father's."

"Well, don't leave us hanging, buddy," Mike appealed.

"You are all familiar with Jung's idea of the *collective unconscious* I'm sure. Good. You know, the same idea floating around with more than one person having it? Well this is a wonderful example, and I'm not only taken back but humbled by it, because here is someone dealing with an idea, a problem that I've been working off and on with for years. Yet he's halfway round the globe from me, no one has ever heard of him, and if my speculation is correct, he's solved it."

"What?"

"Breaking the law of gravity. I won't bore you with details but this configuration, using a series of laser tones, could cause this cylinder to simply float."

"That's where the crystals are to be installed," Dama volunteered.

"Precisely."

"Cut to the chase, Andre, for God's sake."

"It means that the function of the crystals could remain undisturbed even in a major earthquake unless the entire room it's in—which I'm sure is reinforced to withstand a hell of a jolt—is destroyed, this cylinder and its crystal cargo just keep on floating. So, the cylinder has got to be kept in play so to speak. The more difficult and frightening question to me is what happens when the cylinders fall or are destroyed by, say, an earthquake?" He shuddered.

"You mean, are the crystals just a conduit that would be harmless if the whole thing was destroyed or the power shut off?" Jon Lee was slowly, rhythmically tapping his staff against his palm.

"I'd give that a fifty percent chance, Jon Lee, but also, Dama's brother placed some significance on the location of this super-secret missile facility at Kennedy Meadows. Yes, if the crystals are a conduit, it could be directed there and detonate the nuclear and other materials."

Andre sighed. "Yes. As I said…fifty percent…it could go either way."

"So, what are the options?" Mike asked.

Andre's normal jovial demeanor had faded away. "I don't think we can do anything here. Imagine us running to the feds with our story." They all nodded in agreement. "This is science way beyond anything we possess here in the Western Hemisphere."

"Whose fate may right now be shifting from Dama's father to her brother."

Andre shook his head as if too perplexed to fathom that. "I see no options. It would have to be shut down and therefore destroyed."

They looked at each other in the silence. No one seemed to know what to say. Finally, Dama spoke. "I know another way into the Holy City. No guarantees. Long ago, Panjali showed me the button that would destroy the city. He thought it was a joke on me, pretending to push it."

Andre never flinched but Mike and Jon Lee looked surprised. "If you could do that, my dear, and someone could get to the power source without being apprehended or killed, it could be done. But, and this is a very important *but*, like all powerful technologies— and I speculate this one is as powerful as it gets— shutting it down without a failsafe would destroy it so no one else could learn how it was constructed."

"But do you think that would include that chamber in Mt. Noe?" Mike asked.

Andre looked at him for a full moment. "I would assume so."

They were silent again, until, finally, Jon Lee broke it. "We could be running after nothing."

Andre shook both his first finger and head at Jon Lee. "Were that it were so, Jon Lee, but given the actors on stage, and given the display of their technological ability thus far, I think we're looking at something that could pose not just a local threat to us but to the world, because, as I said, those beams can be set down anywhere. My guess is that if shut down and destroyed at the source, the beam as a conduit dies. However, there's still the matter of the crystals which I also think would be rendered harmless since there would be no power source with which to detonate them." He looked at them again. "You all realize of course that if there is power in the crystals themselves, the four of us would have to live out our lives knowing that there was a horrifying source of power, probably capable of destroying everything in sight and beyond, sitting quietly beneath Mt. Noe?" They nodded.

"What can we do then, damn it?" Mike asked.

"Hope that destroying the power source will destroy it all."

"But we would have to fly there and be very lucky." Andre smiled somberly. "I can provide the transportation part. We could leave tomorrow night. Dama should remain here where she'll be safe until you return." He looked fondly at her. "Without you on board, Dama, Jon Lee would be correct, there'd be no reason for making this insane voyage."

Mike picked up the tarp and helped Andre put it back in place. "My guess is that if all the connections we think are in place, isn't somebody pretty damn soon

going to find out about Jon Lee and Dama's
relationship?"

"And, because of me, come looking for you."
There was fear in her eyes as she looked at Jon Lee.

"They probably can't do that in forty-eight
hours. They'll be focused on the installation and only
the two bodyguards saw me. I know they would not tell
on me."

"Nonetheless, time is short. Go, you two bring
what you need. I will make sure Dama has what she
needs. Be back here as early as possible. This is a safe
harbor. If the installation is completed on schedule by
ten tomorrow, then I'll have it tested by 1:00 and we'll
know where the beams are directed. That might tell us
something more. We can be airborne by 2:00 tomorrow.
Now, go with care."

The next morning at 8:00 when Yee Chin went
out to perform his twice daily ritual of sweeping the
gutter sidewalk and steps of the Kiwan, Jon Lee was
sitting in lotus posture against the wall on the porch.
Chin finished his sweeping and went back inside.

Jon Lee sat immobile throughout the day as
students came and went, sometimes bowing, sometimes
tittering. At 5:00, Chin returned to repeat his task, but
Jon Lee remained. He had sat there for eight hours

without food, water or movement. This time, before he opened the door, Chin touched Jon Lee's shoulder with his staff and rising slowly and stiffly, Jon Lee followed him inside.

Sitting by the Koi pond, Yee Chin learned the whole story. "Its shape is darkness because whoever wins, there will be no peace whose pillars are based upon violence. I will be waiting at five in the morning. Until then, open your defenses. Be ready. That dark shape may be coming for you." Jon Lee stood, bowed and left.

There was nothing to do now but wait. He packed his backpack with enough clothing to last a few days. The gun was in a locked drawer by his bed and he opened the drawer and contemplated it. Leaving it where it was, he closed the drawer and locked it.

Out in the kitchen, he stirred up some vegetables and cut up chicken and poured it over a bowl of brown rice. There was no telling when, and if, their next meal would be. He sat on the deck and ate very slowly. It was after 8:00 pm when he finished, cleaned up the dishes, and realized there were still eight hours before picking up his master.

His mind whirled with thoughts of Dama, Mike, Andre, and this unknown destination. Never once did he contemplate his disciplinary hearing in two weeks which he was sure, given those who wanted to get rid of him, would turn his suspension into a dismissal. Finally, around eleven he dropped off to sleep.

At ten to four, the time he would get up, he could feel the strain on his deck beyond the open French doors. The sensation was as if the whole house was shifting that way. The sounds of heavy breathing were followed by a lot of weight shifting from foot to foot. From the moon's reflection, he recognized the big man, Johnny, from Locke's office who still had a bandage on his right ear, and the others behind him he was sure were Dama's bodyguards, Chaudri and Mohamed.

They came in single file through the deck door, down the hall and into his bedroom. Johnny motioned Chaudri to the other side of the bed and Mohamed to its foot. The sleeper hadn't stirred. He put an enormous hand on Jon Lee's throat as Chaudri grasped his legs and Mohamed let him feel the long knife blade against his cheek. "Nothing will happen to you as long as you deliver the girl." Jon Lee tried to turn slightly but the grip on his neck became even tighter.

"She's not here."

"We can see that, but we also know that you can find her for us. You disagree. Then something will happen to you, worse than what you did to me a month ago, I promise."

They felt his body relaxing. They held on. But suddenly Mohamed let out a scream of pain as the knife dropped to the floor and Jon Lee's staff ripped out under Mohamed's chin and curved to squarely connect with the center of Johnny's forehead as they both seemed to crumple in place. He had snapped his feet from Chaudri's grasp who tried frantically to reach the bedroom door, but Jon Lee blocked his way. Chaudri froze, not knowing what to do, but the decision was made for him as he suddenly felt himself, without being pushed, flying towards the back wall of the room, which cracked his collar bone as he hit the wall and the side of a built-in bookcase before falling forward to the floor.

Jon Lee left them where they lay, grabbed his pack and hurried up the brick path to the garage where he backed the Porsche out and idled up the street. As he checked his rearview mirror, a large black town car with two passengers pulled away from the curve, following him. Jon Lee drove casually, not trying to lose the other car and at 4:30 he came slowly up Jackson and Yee Chin climbed in easily. "I've got someone behind me."

"Go through Golden Gate Park, out by the old windmill," Yee Chin said without looking back." They drove out California through Pacific Heights and into the Richmond District where he went left on 26th and into the park. They wound back and forth until they reached the main road and went right.

The windmill was just a mile or so away when Yee Chin told him to accelerate slightly. "When we reach it, turn into the leaves, the ground around the windmill is hard."

Locke's people, Robert and Al, had no idea what happened. The plan was to pick up the Jap, force him to take them to the Arab's sister, pick her up and dump him. Mr. Locke had been very specific, "You can rough him up, but don't kill him."

"What the hell are they doing?" Al asked as he accelerated to keep up.

"What the hell happened to our guys is my question. I told Mr. Locke this wasn't gonna work, but Big Johnny has always gotta have the last word. All we can do now is follow him and the other Jap or Chinaman he picked up in Chinatown. Maybe he's going for the girl. What the hell, he's turning in by that windmill."

"Don't lose him!"

They could barely make out the Porsche's tail lights as the dead leaves it stirred up began to partially block their vision. Jon Lee went around once, then twice, but on the third time, they lost sign of him and plunged through the leaves to the back side. As they came around there was a man in a black robe standing directly in front of them. There was no way to avoid hitting him, even though Robert tried desperately to swerve to the outside. Then, suddenly and without

248

warning the car was rising and tilting, the passenger's side skidding along on the leaves until it began to roll end over end toward a dead pine tree.

      Designate 8 was standing nervously looking out as the sun turned the bay into a sheet of silver foil. His former escort, Rasheed, had called him at seven, telling him to turn on his monitor and be prepared to speak with Esse at 9:00 sharp. He called his office and had to cancel an important financial and political meeting. Waiting for anything had always made him uneasy. The monitor sat on the largest section of his bookcase next to the living room window. Rasheed and someone else had come to install it when the planning had begun for the UN *Week of Peace* in which Designate 8 would play a vital part. This way, he and Esse could communicate directly with each other. The green button came on and instantly Esse's face and upper body appeared on the screen. There wasn't the usual smile on his face. In fact, Designate 8 thought he looked very sad.

      "Good morning, my friend. Ah, I see out your window that it is a beautiful day in your city."

      "Yes, it is. But, if you don't mind me saying so, you look sad and tired. Is everything all right?"

      Esse signed and shook his head. "I should have guessed that fathers cannot hide their feelings from each other." He hesitated, looking away from the camera. "My daughter, Dama, who is in your city to help the contingency from our part of the world, she…. she has disappeared."

Having two grown daughters of his own, and being such a public person, this too had been a fear he still lived with. "Sir, I can help you. You know my connections could quickly enlarge and speed up an investigation into her whereabouts. Please, let me help."

Esse raised his hand and smiled weakly. "Thank you my friend, your continued loyalty and support is all I ask. She was not kidnapped, I know that. My people are working on this. I wouldn't want the American population to know that one of the speakers at the UN celebration was before them under such a cloud. I am confident that she will be found shortly and the wheels are in motion to achieve that right now.

No, what I needed from you is a fax of the timetable of the events for the opening session of the meeting, especially the first afternoon and evening, including all security precautions. If you could send me that in detail by noon today I would be grateful, and if I need more I'll let you know. You have made miracles in bringing this together and I'm sure all the delegates will tell you that personally."

"Thank you, but…."

"No, all will be well soon, I am confident. Have a beautiful day, my friend."

The screen went blank and the green light faded away. Why did he always feel so uneasy after talking with this man who was more a close acquaintance than a stranger now? He went to the wet bar, took a swig from the Cutty Sark, brushed his teeth again and hurried out.

Chapter Seventeen

Upon seeing his comrades fall, the rage of the warlord Khilma was unleashed, and he led a frenzied attack on the monk. It lasted for more than two hours as wave upon wave of barbarians surged forward onto the overhang only to fall with a single blow from the monk's bamboo staff or just the wave of his hand, vanishing in screams of despair as they hurled downward into the canyon's razor sharp darkness.

When it ended, nearly the entire army, numbering over a hundred-fifty barbarians, had died with just a handful fleeing down the mountain and away on a single ship. Only Wo Chin and the wind remained. Without looking back, he struggled over the rock and up the path. He was covered with dirt, bruises and blood.

As he came through the monastery gate, the cook and villagers rushed out of the temple hall, astonished that he was still alive. 'You may go home now' was all he said as he walked slowly to his tiny cell.

8:00 a.m., Sunday, May 25th: Mecca

They had been heading due east, crossing Egypt with the Suez Canal below like a dark length of rope touching the Arabian Sea to the south and the eastern Mediterranean Sea to the north. Andre had just received landing instructions from the Mecca tower and the Lear 36 banked left across an orange sun half risen from the far desert.

It had been an uneventful flight, but the weight of their mission was already showing on all but Yee Chin's and Jon Lee's faces, who had either slept or meditated during most of the flight. As they landed and began taxiing to the private plane area away from the main terminal, Andre's voice came over the intercom. "All safe, but this runway looks like a county road that never makes the repair calendar. Glad we're landing in light and hope that's when we'll leave."

He was motioned to a mark on the tarmac and he turned off the engines but kept the air-conditioning going. He opened the hatch and spoke to a man in a turban then got back on board. "They're turning us around and towing us backward into the hanger. I'm impressed that they can give her a complete service right where she'll be berthing until we leave. Once the plane was in the hangar facing out, Andre shut off the air-conditioner and opened the door. Under cover of the hanger and given the early hour, it was still mild and a soft breeze blew into the cabin.

Without speaking, everyone checked their packs, water, dried foods, passports (Andre had to *create* ones for Mike and Jon Lee) and other gear before they gathered around a table up against the rear bulkhead. Andre had put over 25,000 hours on it, but the interior looked as if no one had ever used it. He shifted his great bulk into a swivel chair next to the table. "Well, who will begin? Dama, I believe you would be the appropriate one."

"The train we take leaves from the station in the old part of the city, not far from this airport. I'm afraid it is not well maintained, but it will take us to where we must go in the desert. Andre was able to find schedules on his laptop. Not that they've always adhered to them, but we missed the first train at 1:00 this morning and now must wait for the one tonight at 6:00. Just two runs a day to the mines and what's left of the oil out there.

"It shouldn't take more than half an hour to find the entrance and then another half hour, assuming we aren't captured or.... we can be at the main power source which I've always called *the deep hum*."

"Well, never fear, I'll be there to short-circuit the thing and, in the event I'm not, one thing will occur; you will need transportation out." He laughed.

"We will be fine, Dr. Dumand. We will be fine," Yee Chin repeated.

Andre gave him a double take and raised his eyebrows. "But, Master Chin, I…"

"Sir, you were not meant for desert travel." Everyone had to laugh, even Andre.

"Well, I finally find my true value, chauffeur."

"No disrespect intended, Doctor, but should we need to exit quickly…. you understand? It is better that you remain here ready to leave immediately upon our return."

"Oh, well." Andre signed.

"Perhaps next time, Andre," Mike consoled.

Jon Lee stood and stretched. "Well, we've got all day."

They found a taxi and Dama took them on a riding tour of the various shrines and other points of interest. Andre, especially, savored a traditional meal in a hotel that Dama said was still run by the British, whose gardens and fountains they walked among afterwards. At 4:00 they returned to the plane and said their goodbyes to Andre.

"Maybe we're just damn fools who've let our egos get out of hand, carrying us into some Disney World version of reality." Mike speculated.

"Would the authorities have believed any of this, Michael?" Andre asked.

"Sorry, Mike, but isn't that kind of what a Pulitzer is?" Jon Lee smiled.

Mike nodded and seemed to relax. "Point well taken, but still…."

Yee Chin had been polite but mostly silent during their trip to town, but he spoke now. "In the line of Zahu, the only line, the one from which I come, there was once a boy in the 12th Century, far frailer than we as a group, who met odds that surely to him were as overwhelming as these are to us."

"And what was the outcome Master Chin?" Andre asked with quiet humility.

Yee Chin only smiled. "You will learn that if we succeed." Everyone laughed.

9:00 p.m., Saturday, May 24th:
Palace of the Legion of Honor

There were lights in all the trees that lined the curving road that led up to San Francisco's Palace of the Legion of Honor, where at this late hour only one car made its way to the glass and marble front entry. Designate 8 opened the door of the limousine himself and went directly along the lighted path lined with shrubs and flowers to the entrance. The local Marine Reserve was providing security, and two Marine sergeants came to attention as he approached. "Good evening, sir."

"Good evening." He handed them his VIP badge and they returned it with a salute. "Just checking some last-minute details."

"Do you need any help with the lights, sir?"

"No, I'll be fine. Thank you."

Through another open court, he crossed over and entered the main room where the front had a curved platform slightly raised with the UN symbol and flags from all the represented countries. The current members of the Security Council would be sitting there. In the front was an area cordoned off with a gold braded rope where local dignitaries sat with the representatives of fifty nations who would be attending. Behind this area were enough seats for at least two hundred more who had been invited by special invitation only. The entire room looked out through a wall of glass onto the grounds and the lighted trees that spread out in the slow decline of the knoll. Glancing out the window, he thought about the unnerving intelligence report from a couple of days ago. It hadn't been confirmed, but there was some vague threat from an unidentified source in the Middle East protesting the UN meeting and vowing to take vengeance against it. Lord, he thought, they certainly wouldn't be trying to plant a suicide bomber among the help, or even a diplomat, would they? The Marine guard had been doubled anyway and everyone would be screened at the entrance. He repeated to himself several times that everything would be fine, but he wasn't convinced.

He went under the rope to the second row where his seat was on the aisle, and sat down slowly and wearily. Everything was ready. The mural behind the Security Council table still smelled of wet paint but he was assured that it would be dry by tomorrow evening at 8:00 when, after the reception in the gallery from 5:00 to 6:30 and dinner at 7:00, the ceremony would begin. The mural had been a very difficult task to achieve because it drew on the services of artists from twenty-four countries who had come the week prior to paint it. At one point, even a fistfight broke out between two of them, but by yesterday afternoon the last paint had been peacefully applied and the astonishing array of colors and symbols was breathtaking. Why was there always such confusion between personal agendas and just being human? He'd always hoped there was a difference, but experience had taught him the opposite. Maybe Esse's way was the only way.

What he hadn't been able to figure out was how Esse was going to appear on that wall, now that the mural was in place. Designate 8 had felt a sudden tremor of fear when he'd gotten an advance copy of the program and found no mention of Esse, but Esse had assured him half a dozen times in the past few days that his appearance would be a complete surprise and no one must know of it in advance. That concerned him too.

Something cracked behind him and he turned suddenly. But in the dim safety lights he saw nothing. He got up and went back under the rope. Before he was halfway down the aisle, he was almost trotting, and he kept at it across the open court and down the long hall to the entrance until he saw the guards and forced himself to slow to a walk. Designate 8 suddenly realized that he had no control over what was going to happen tomorrow night, when all his life he'd been the one in complete control. He nodded to the guards and hurried down the steps and into his car. Before the driver had reached the decorative iron front gate, the twitch in Designate 8's cheek had come back to life.

12:07 a.m., Monday May 27th:
Mecca and the Desert

The old station must have been one of the first ever built in the city, because when they stepped into the bleached and brittle wood waiting area it was like entering a parallel universe, a place left utterly behind by the force of modern ways. At 6:30, the train remained empty and Dama went to the ticket window.

"They are having trouble finding the second engineer," was all she could glean from the station master who acted as if this happened so often as to be a part of his daily routine.

It wasn't until just before nine that the boilers were fired up and they boarded the old relic. Windows were broken and missing, and the floor and benches looked like that hadn't been swept or cleaned for years. The only light came from large candles at the front and rear of the car. These were covered with antique glass bulbs upon which insects had left their dusty impressions.

In this light the passengers took on the look of shadowy impressions that kept changing with the shifts of the car as the train moved along the ancient tracks deeper into the night. Besides themselves, there had been only a woman with three children and two boys about sixteen who looked like they were, for the first time, going off to work in the mines or remaining oil fields at the end of the line. An eerie silence of fatigue and apprehension fell over them as the breeze carried in the dry, irritating smell of coal and wood smoke. Jon Lee sat the whole journey with his arm around Dama, Yee Chin had pulled his legs up in a meditative posture and Mike leaned against the bench, looking out into the desert night.

The train stopped once and Dama and Jon Lee got off. As the train took on water she looked carefully around. "This is too soon. These are not the palms. Mine grew in a semi-circle."

It was approaching midnight when the train slowed and stopped again for water. Here the pond was wide and the palms encircling it looked much healthier. Dama looked out the window, smiled, exclaiming, "This is the place my father made."

They stood in the deep black silence with only an occasional rustle of a palm frond overhead and the blanket of stars as their only light. "Dawn comes a little before 4:00. We should try to rest until then."

"Are you sure this is the place, Dama?" Mike asked.

She touched his arm. "I'm positive, Mike. Look where the palm is missing. Abyase received a severe spanking for making it die. I don't know why we never planted another."

Jon Lee took her pack and put it next to his. "It seems we're glad you didn't."

"How much time do you figure?" Mike was looking at the marine green glow of his watch dial.

"If all goes well and this implant in my hand still functions, we should be inside by five." Dama replied.

"The one thing we haven't talked about is whether we think Esse's beamed image at the UN thing is a timetable we're racing against." Mike continued. "If that's so, with the eleven-hour difference we'll only have a two-hour window once inside, because the

261

meeting starts at 8:00 yesterday evening their time which'll make it seven this morning for us."

No one spoke as they settled down in the sand. "Seven is the future, Mike." Yee Chin said quietly. "We are here now. Rest in the present." He drew his jacket around him like a blanket and lay back on the pack as the others did the same.

5:15 p.m., Sunday, May 26th:
Palace of the Legion of Honor

Shelia was wearing a black floor length gown that was sleeveless and gathered at the neck, simple and elegant. She wore no jewelry except a plain gold bracelet and a silver banded ring with one rough cut piece of jade in the center. The guests were starting to arrive in a parade of limousines. For the first time since she'd arrived an hour before to do a final security walk through with the Marine captain, she began to relax a little. They were taking the threat of a terrorist attack from earlier that week very seriously, and she felt more assured after her tour of the building and grounds with him, but that seemed minor to other concerns that refused to leave her.

She took a half glass of white wine out through the glass doors in the auditorium and stood alone on the patio. It was the meeting with Charles Locke just after the little girl's murder, and the picture of her that the

Chronicle ran that haunted her. She'd arrived by motor launch and he'd greeted her at his dock. Over a lunch of fresh, hot French rolls and a shrimp salad and wine, she'd laid bare her feelings.

"Was the child's murder related to this project, Charles?"

"Those are not the questions a candidate for mayor should be asking, Shelia." He examined the large shrimp on his fork before putting it slowly into his mouth.

"I've done a lot of things I'm not proud of, but something like this...."

"Did getting the mayor to sign onto the Corfu Village project bother you?"

"No."

"You've been playing the political game for several years, my dear. You understand how it works. I wouldn't be enjoying any of this," he motioned with his arm to their surroundings, "unless I'd learned the game long ago."

"The child wasn't a game, Charles. At least, not for me."

It wasn't just his words but his expression when he replied, "The game gets dirty sometimes, Shelia." There had been not a trace of emotion on his face or in his tone. He could have been talking as if the little girl had been killed in a movie or video game.

Voices behind and to her left shook her from that lunch meeting. The inner court was filling up as people drank, talked and sampled the appetizers from silver trays passed around by members of the catering staff. No expense had been spared. She had fought for that.

Down on the road, Charles Locke and his wife were getting out of his silver Rolls Royce. He knew that at fifty-six, he cut a sporting and handsome figure: tall and lean with his thick, nearly white hair perfectly cut and combed. He saw Shelia standing dreamily at the top of the knoll on the patio. He waved but she didn't acknowledge it.

They were now locked together, so long as either should live, in a kind of perversion of marriage. Nothing the holy fathers of his church would have approved but, nonetheless, a marriage of interests.

After they'd been scanned, his wife saw two friends and he excused himself to find Shelia. She was standing just as still, staring at the trees and grassy knoll.

"Much of what I see has the touch of Shelia Vernin," Charles Locke said, coming up behind her. He kissed her cheek. "Very impressive, Madame Mayor."

She laughed and looked up at him. "I'll believe it when I see it, Charles."

"As well you should. As a man of his word I can say that the wheels are beginning to turn." She patted his arm. "Where's the mayor himself?"

"He should be here soon. The dramatic entrance and all that. You know how he is."

"Yes, and how much he depends on you. I want you to know that I don't think the Corfu project would have gone through without your nod to him. You won't be sorry, Shelia."

She looked out into the garden and across the lawn as the dignitaries continued to stream up the path. "I can't get that little girl out of my mind, Charles."

"Nor I Shelia. It was senseless, a revenge killing gone wrong."

"No, Charles. The investigation didn't show Mr. Dobkovnic to have any criminal associations. He was never an accountant. Just a tanner."

"And that's where it should end. It was a horrible mistake."

"We better start to mingle, Charles. People believe rumors so easily." He looked at her questioningly and nodded. "I'll see you at dinner."

"I'll mind my manners with the mayor." He smiled and walked toward the sea of smiling and laughing faces. The afternoon fishing on his dock with two of his grandchildren surfaced. He did feel a sense of remorse for the child. He would have stopped it if he could. But, he assured himself, it has become part of

265

the momentum, one of the strands that had broken. Homer Thween should never have been given such power. It was he who should have died on those steps.

3:40-5:10 a.m., Monday, May 27th:
The Desert and the Holy City

Dawn came early. Only Yee Chin and Jon Lee had slept. They climbed to the top of a dune and Mike opened his compass. He pointed. "That's just a little west of north."

They hadn't walked more than twenty minutes when Dama stopped and felt the back of her hand. "It's still working. I'm feeling the pain a little now." Jon Lee took her pack and hitched it over his other shoulder. "It's working, that's very good." She managed a delicate smile.

But in another forty-five minutes it was no longer just a little pain, because Dama was massaging her hand and arm and it had begun to register on her face. She stumbled and they helped her up. "Not…not far. Just there," she pointed with her other hand. They helped her up the broad and slow rising dune. "Jon Lee, look there, please." He probed with his staff. At the height of the dune it hit something hard, and he and Mike dug away the sand. It was the metal disk just as she had described, like the hatch of a submarine, and in its center was a round thick glasslike surface with a blue light deep inside it. Dama waved the back of her hand over it and they all stood clear as a whirring sound began, followed by a swish and a click as the hatch opened enough for Jon Lee and Mike to lift it up.

Her pain seemed to be increasing. They moved quickly inside and down the ladder, their feet on each step making a grinding sound like sand on metal. Once inside, Dama pressed her hand against a similar blue light in glass and the hatch sealed itself instantly. She leaned back against the wall for several minutes to catch her breath. "It goes away as soon as it's shut. Come, this way."

"Won't that trigger an alarm, Dama?" Mike asked.

"I don't know, Mike. I never thought of that when I was with my father."

They hurried down the earthen passage with Yee Chin and Jon Lee taking the lead. In moments, they'd reached the high, broad warehouse. As if in unison, the bamboo staffs rose and the two men stepped onto the hard, man-made floor. Chin touched Jon Lee's arm and he glanced over at his master. Quietly the old man said, "This is your Wang Ny, Jon Lee, or mine, although the lives involved are many more than that small village." Jon Lee did something he'd always wanted to do but never dared, he gently pressed his hand against Yee Chin's shoulder.

They began to move forward, keeping close to containers and walls whenever they could, but at one point they had to traverse an open space about thirty feet long between containers. Mike whispered over Jon Lee's shoulder. "It's too quiet."

"Way too quiet for a warehouse, Mike."

They had nearly traversed the open space when suddenly the wall opened and a group of fierce looking men carrying everything from swords to automatic weapons burst into the warehouse. The largest one in front was Rasheed. When he saw Dama his face dropped momentarily. But the ferocity quickly returned.

Jon Lee gave a quick glance at Yee Chin but his master's staff had vanished.

As they hurried the group at gunpoint through the warehouse, she tried to speak to him, expressing her sadness at his betrayal of their father, but Rasheed would not look at her or respond. His rigid jaw and tightly closed lips showed her the face of consuming anger.

No one had been searched; it was as if the thought of searching anyone in the Holy City no longer existed in Rasheed's mind, so shocked was he at finding her. The room they came to was like the warehouse, but instead of containers, it had a series of jail like cells along both walls whose roofs were also barred, giving each the look of cages. There were only two in the front occupied and one in the rear where a very elderly man lay on his cot. He rose slowly as they came toward him.

Dama cried out, "Burta, my teacher. What is this cruelty?" She asked Rasheed.

"He has challenged your father's vision. He speaks lies to our people, saying that having the power to destroy is not the way to peace." He motioned to a guard who opened the cell and Rasheed shoved her inside. "There, you may keep your teacher company as a fellow traitor!"

The others were put in a cell with four cots. "I go now to tell your father, Dama. This is a bitter time for us all." Rasheed turned and walked out.

There were only two guards and a monitoring system whose cameras were attached to the top of the cells and constantly roved the area in front of them. Dama's cell was just across from theirs. "This is my dear teacher, Burta." He acknowledged them with a humble nod. "What can we do?" The guard motioned her to move to the cot and silenced her in Arabic.

"Good question." Mike spoke in a whisper. "We're dead."

5:30-6:30 a.m., Monday, May 26th:
The Holy City

Esse was standing by the water of the small pond in his quarters. Abyase stood a foot from his father but they weren't looking at each other. "I am sorry about my sister, father. I don't know what to say."

Esse patted his son's back gently. "She is alive and has apparently run off with this police lieutenant. I don't think she means me any harm. I will always believe that she believes in our mission, our vision."

"If I may speak on that matter, father. I think her time in London exposed her too long to western ways, to this vile feminism that is everywhere, turning women from the nurturers of children and family matters into aggressive heathens." Esse started to object. "Please, let me finish. Perhaps that isn't true in her case but suddenly abandoning our mission just days before all was complete." He looked directly at his father. "I know how hard it was to bring everyone home, not knowing about her."

"She will return to us." Esse paused. "In time. But now we must focus on the task at hand. In less than one hour we gather in the laboratory to transmit our message to the United Nations meeting."

"And I will tell you what I have already. I do not agree with the velvet glove approach to these barbarians. They defile their own precious water, their forests, their land and each other in the name of their God, money. They will not heed what you say unless you instantly and very graphically demonstrate it somewhere in Sector 1, whether that be Los Angeles, in Canada, down in Mexico or, most immediately in some part of San Francisco. They need to see a part of a city laid waste with the inhabitants unharmed, and if it were within my power I would do just the opposite, because unless they know fear and eminent death, they will pay no attention to your soft tones for peace, believe me, father!" Abayse had begun to walk along the shore of the pond, back and forth in agitation.

"My son, I am the one who created this city with the vision of peace. I must take responsibility for this first step."

"I am only telling you my opinion. I think yours and the present council's gets us nowhere. I will stand by your side when you speak, but you know my mind."

"And I have never understood how opposite our visions…."

The wall to Esse's quarters suddenly opened and Rasheed, wild eyed, entered. "My father, please excuse the intrusion but the secret hatch alarm was triggered. Please, forgive me for this, but…. Dama was among the intruders!"

Yee Chin was sitting next to Mike on a cot. He said gently, "We only appear to have died." Mike looked at him, puzzled.

"We could have disarmed them," Jon Lee interjected, "but that would have only brought a greater force."

"They are now dissipated." Yee Chin said.

"They think we're contained and in an hour Esse is supposed to speak to the UN meeting. They'll deal with us later. Now we're ready to continue."

Yee Chin slowly lay down on the cot and Jon Lee felt his forehead. "Dama, tell the guards he has a fever and needs water."

Both guards came to the cell but one stood about ten feet away and clicked off the safety latch on his automatic weapon. The guard spoke to Dama. "He wants you and Mike to move away from Yee Chin. He will set the water on the table. He says if anyone moves the other one will kill all of you."

The guard very slowly unlocked the cell and brought the water in and set it cautiously down on the table. He had just about closed the cell door and was reaching for his key when the other one with the automatic weapon let out a loud, shattering cry as his head snapped violently back and he fell to the ground. As the one at the door turned to see what had happened, a piece of wood fell to the floor next to the guard and before he could turn back to lock the cell he felt a strong hand on his wrist as he was pulled against the bars and knocked unconscious. They hurried out and opened the cell with Burta and Dama. Jon Lee retrieved his staff, and they ran for the passage.

They heard voices from a distance but had to slow their pace as Burta limped along. He kept smiling at Dama in the joy of seeing her alive. "They said yesterday that you had died."

She threw out her arms. "Well, I haven't." She stopped to hug him.

"Dama, what can you do? I fear the worst now, because those who are still my friends and former students tell me that Abyase plans to do something drastic when Esse speaks today."

"We are trying to reach the power source." Mike said. "If we could shut it down or dismantle it, that won't happen."

Burta shook his head. "To shut off the power is simple, sir, but it is well guarded. And if you managed to turn it off, it will self-destruct this whole city, like a giant earthquake!" That was how it was built. So, you have a choice: you gamble that Esse still holds the power, and many say he no longer does, or you shut it down. If you shut it down, then the city dies a violent death."

"And the world lives." Mike interrupted.

"Yes. That is the gamble and the choice. Given what I have learned and given that an old and trusted servant like myself has been jailed, I think your choice is clear, but remember, you will die with the city." He paused for breath. "I am very old and will die soon anyway, but all of you except Master Chin have the real beauty of life ahead." He gazed at Dama.

"Burta I love you so, but we have no choice." Dama wiped a tear from her eye. "Please, be our guide."

He looked at each of them as if it would be the last time. "As you wish, Dama, it's not far but we can't take the normal route. My way is longer and my age makes it even longer than that, but it is doubtful that we will encounter anyone. We must go quickly. The guards may have regained consciousness by now or we were seen on the monitors and no corridor in the city will be safe for us soon."

They turned into a corridor and left the warehouse. It was as silent as when they'd first entered.

7:55p.m., Sunday, May 26th:
Palace of the Legion of Honor

Designate 8 still felt a deep apprehension of what lay ahead this evening, but his public face was in place as the dinner ended and everyone began to file into the auditorium. What if some maniac suddenly detonated himself in the middle of the program? He tried hard to put that out of his mind as he received compliments for himself personally and the committee for the orchestra that had played beautifully during dinner and for the excellent food, service and dedicated work that had made the celebration a reality. The rows of gold leaf and brocade chairs were nearly filled as he came down the aisle greeting people. There was even a brief applause which he acknowledged as he sat humbly down in the second row beyond the gold rope.

At exactly eight o'clock when the lights dimmed and the glass wall made the lighted garden into a fairyland, he cautiously glanced around. But nothing had changed since the previous evening except the press cameras and reporters who were not allowed beyond the last row of chairs. Besides the Secretary General and California Senator Barbara Boxer, the guest speaker, the rest of the curved table contained the Security Council members and the Under Secretary of State. His political connections had definitely paid off and he smiled.

The Secretary General rose to thunderous applause, graciously acknowledged them and began to speak. "Ladies and gentlemen, most distinguished guests from around the world, welcome to the fiftieth anniversary of your United Nations." There was more applause. The Secretary had barely launched into his remarks when Designate 8 began to feel warm. At first, he thought it might be the excitement and the wine but then the Secretary took out his handkerchief and patted his forehead and cheeks, interrupting himself to ask if others were feeling as hot as he did.

7:00 a.m., Monday, May 27th:
The Holy City

Burta had led them through the shadows and now they could hear Dama's *big hum*, a short distance away. "There are only two entrances. You must either go directly through the main one or the tunnel just down this corridor about half a kilometer. That would be the best route but also the most dangerous."

"Why?" Yee Chin asked.

"There is an electrical circuit that runs through the tunnel that can be activated if there is any sign of movement. It is the last line of defense against an intruder. Only once did someone enter there without permission and all that was left of him was a handful of ash. Even his bones had disintegrated when they found his remains."

"The tunnel then," Chin said. He turned to Jon Lee and held out his hand, pointing to Jon Lee's staff which he extended to him. Yee Chin took it, placing his own, worn as smooth as glass, into his student's palm. "Take them and leave." Jon Lee knew that to protest would have been a useless gesture.

"You don't know the way Master Chin." Dama stepped forward. "Burta is too feeble to help. I must do it."

"No, Dama, no!" Jon Lee turned her, holding her shoulders, forcing her to look up at him.

8:10 p.m., Sunday, May 26th:
Palace of the Legion of Honor

When everyone acknowledged that they too were hot, he joked, "Perhaps we're all a bit nervous about our next fifty years in the United Nations," and asked the maintenance people to see what the problem was. Some of the garden doors were opened but even with that the heat was becoming more intense.

The scream directly behind Designate 8 was so high and frantic that he thought someone was having a heart attack, but when he turned the woman was pointing to the mural behind the Secretary. Beginning at the top, the paint had begun to run, slowly at first, mixing with those below it until the entire wall was running with paint as the scenes of two dozen artists became nothing more than a surrealistic river of color flowing down onto the stage. It took less than five minutes for it to become a blank white wall again.

Designate 8 could feel his cheek just beginning to twitch and he'd left his flask at home. What could he do? People were standing, some ready to exit, but they stopped in place when the wall came to life with the picture of Esse from the shoulders up. His smile was so serene that even in the midst of the general anxiety it had a calming effect and, as if hypnotized, people began to sit down as air-conditioning began cooling the room.

"Hello my friends, and welcome. I come in peace, I bid you all, peace."

7:10 a.m., Monday, May 27th:
The Holy City

"This is my family's horrible creation and if I must die with it then that's my responsibility. My father has set in motion what the poet Eliot once said was 'the right deed for the wrong reason.' It is beyond control now. And in Abyase's hands, no one knows what madness may be unleashed." She reached up, holding Jon Lees' head and kissing him passionately. "There is no choice," she said, forcing herself out of his embrace.

Mike hugged her, and she turned to lead the way. He had all he could do to hold Jon Lee back but finally his friend went limp and they turned to follow Burta back to the tunnel and the desert.

Dama and Yee Chin reached the corridor with the tunnel entrance into the city's power source but there were two guards on either side of it. Yee Chin motioned her to get down and he hurried past her

278

around the edge of the corner. There was complete silence for a moment and then the sound of someone falling. Yee Chin motioned her forward. The guards lay across their weapons in the corridor and they stepped over them.

They peered inside. The tunnel was about five feet in diameter and lined with a chrome looking substance. He turned to Dama. "This is where it ends. Go now. Hurry. Go to Jon Lee."

"No, Master Chin. This is my responsibility."

He put one foot up in the tunnel. "Go, Dama. This is not your karma." Then he was moving quickly and soundlessly in the tunnel. She watched him disappear around a curve and waited as if frozen in place. She lifted one leg and rested it on the chrome lip, ready to follow him.

8:20 p.m., Sunday, May 26th:
The Palace of the Legion of Honor

The stillness, but for Esse's voice, was immense. No one even coughed. It was as if they'd been frozen in time as Esse spoke in lyrical tones. Everything he said sounded so rational, so right for the world.

The doors had been secured with Marines on the patio and in the rear. The grounds were being searched for bombs and possible terrorists. Designate 8 wanted a drink badly, but wanted out of there even more. Even the thought of ten million dollars deposited in four locations around the world seemed meaningless and distant, and he hadn't the vaguest notion as to why he felt that way.

He'd been staring out the windows at the guards, ramrod straight with weapons held across their chests, when suddenly the audience seemed to gasp in unison. When he looked up his cheek began to twitch worse than it ever had and he thought he might faint.

7:22 a.m., Monday, May 27th:
The Holy City

Yee Chin saw the end of the tunnel about twenty feet ahead, and the room with its black panel in front of which two men in white coats sat. He hesitated as he heard excited voices suddenly enter the room.

Rasheed, sweating profusely, had entered with a security force when they'd notified the main laboratory where Esse had been speaking that someone had breached the tunnel. He signaled the men to be silent and looked across the room where the tunnel entrance stood barely fifteen feet away. He motioned the security team to stand in front of the two technicians.

Let this infidel come. Perhaps, he hoped and prayed, it was the one who had taken Dama from him, the only woman he had ever felt affection for in his life.

All he had to do was show himself and he would be no more. Dama may be gone but revenge would be had and be just!

Rasheed glanced quickly around. No one carried an automatic weapon, because they were forbidden, in case of an accident, anywhere near the main power terminals or other sensitive areas in the city. Rasheed reached over and placed his hand on a red button on the panel where the technicians sat. They waited in total silence. Even the tunnel seemed silent.

Then, just as Yee Chin's form appeared at the entrance, Rasheed pressed the button, and the tunnel ignited in a firestorm of electrical charges, throwing Yee Chin over its chrome lip on to the floor.

Rasheed smiled. He would make this one die slowly, painfully, without mercy. But the smile vanished. Somehow, under some power that could not be human, the man was moving, lifting himself and leaning back against the wall. His shirt was burnt away and he had massive burns on his chest, face and arms, and one leg looked as if he could barely stand on it.

Yee Chin stood quietly, weaving ever so slightly, as he surveyed the small room. Rasheed could not help feel a sense of admiration and respect for someone as close to death as this man was who had managed to stand and face an impossible enemy of five men armed with swords. But there he was.

And then Rasheed took a step back in utter horror as did the others, because the man's right arm had begun to rise as he moved away from the wall with one leg almost dragging. His right hand, now across his chest, was holding something that looked like a piece of bamboo.

Yee Chin stopped just five feet from the five who Rasheed told to circle the small, nearly lifeless man that stood before him. This one was not her lover. Just an old man, now weak and small.

Rasheed's voice had a sudden high pitch to it as he shouted at the men to begin moving around the ragged figure who stood as if dead on his feet, only the eyes moved until they came to rest on Rasheed. He suddenly retreated behind the technicians and pressed up against the panel. The eyes would not leave him. He felt as if they were uncovering every sin, every short coming of his life and laying it before him. He was furious and his voice seemed to fill the room as if come unbeckoned, as if he had no control of it as he shouted in the foreigner's tongue, "Kill him!" The air was filled with swords.

Then the smell of blood and cries of agony pierced the silence as Rasheed tried in vain to push himself further back against the panel, as if seeking refuge within its cold, dark fiber. His body was dripping with sweat and had begun to shake uncontrollably. For the first time in his life, he knew and felt the grip of deep, primal fear sweep over him. The man in rags was still standing and limping towards him.

8:25 p.m., Sunday, May 26th:
Palace of the Legion of Honor

Esse was roughly pulled from the screen and an enraged Abyase now stood where his father had been on the anemic white wall. While Esse had donned western clothing, Abyase stood in the oatmeal robe with his arms defiantly folded across his chest. The scabbard of a large sword had been wedged through his sash. "You are the demons of the world! You have slaughtered the innocent and profited from the meek so you can understand only one language, the language of violence and fear. That is why I can no longer allow my father's innocence and faith in demons like you to continue. You are the heathens of the world and your language is money and death. If there will be world peace it will be on my terms and I am now prepared to show you just how powerful my resolve...." The screen went blank.

People were screaming everywhere. A woman to his left appeared to have fainted and a Marine was giving a foreign diplomat CPR near the windows. It was chaos. Through a loudspeaker someone was shouting, "Be calm. The grounds are secure. Be calm, please. You will be able to leave now. Don't panic, please."

Designate 8 staggered toward the door with the others. As he neared it he looked back over the heads of the crowd behind. Their faces were blank, as if they had already died but their bodies kept up an unrelenting momentum.

7:30 a.m. - 10:30 a.m., Monday, May 27th: Desert and Mecca

Burta bade them farewell at the steps to the hatch. "My life needs to end now. I would not want to die away from family and friends." His hand hovered over the blue light.

They'd climbed up and out into the early desert sun, trotting as fast as they dared in the morning heat until they reached the oasis. After washing up, Mike fell exhausted into the shadow of a palm and Jon Lee sat down beside him. "This is what you get for dragging an old guy along." Mike smiled. Jon Lee nodded but said nothing. Mike reached over and touched his shoulder. "Maybe she'll make it out, somehow."

Jon Lee shook his head in doubt and lay back on his pack. The silence enveloped them. A few minutes later when Mike was almost asleep, Jon Lee nudged him, motioning to stay down.

Coming over the edge of the last dune they saw what looked like at least two dozen men armed with swords and automatic weapons running towards the oasis from the direction of the secret entrance to the Holy City. As soon as they saw Mike and Jon Lee, they charged, firing wildly.

Jon Lee pressed Mike closer to the sand. "Don't move, Mike. Don't raise your head." But Mike had raised up on one elbow to see where Jon Lee was going, and almost instantly his shoulder was filled with the sharpest pain he'd ever felt in his life. Instinctively, he grasped for it. It was wet, and smelled of blood.

The men who were charging down the dune were members of the elite force that protected Esse and his family. They'd received training equivalent to and beyond that of U.S. Navy Seals, Army Rangers and Air Force Pathfinders, and their focus now was on the shape that was darting between the palms which partially encircled the oasis pond.

It seemed impossible that the amount of automatic fire they were applying had not at least wounded him as he went from tree to tree. Then, he'd suddenly stopped, and the leader motioned for his men to cease firing and drop to the desert floor. They waited, catching their breath. The leader assumed that this man or the one with him must have stolen away Esse's beautiful daughter. But soon he would be dead. And if either survived, they could be taken back for questioning.

The leader and his men began to relax a little as they waited. It was only a matter of time and victory was theirs. The infidel would be taught the power of Esse and, now, the even more fierce power of Abyase, who would be pleased if they could bring at least one of them back alive. But then the man stepped slowly from behind a palm. He was still alive! The leader shouted to hold their fire. The man took a few steps away from the tree. He had removed his shirt and was barefoot.

Motioning for them to arise slowly, the leader was about to dispatch three men, under cover of the others, down the dune to subdue this evil standing with his arms apart, as if signaling his own surrender. What was it he held in his right hand? The leader took out his binoculars. It looked like nothing but a length of wood. He laughed to himself. Then he moved the binoculars to the man's face. Odd. Instead of the fear he expected to see, the face had the faint edge of a smile and his features appeared quite calm.

The three, weapons at the ready, were halfway down the dune when the man with the stick closed his arms across his chest and seemed to vanish in the sand that rose around him as he began to twirl, over and over until there was nothing where he stood but a funnel, like the eye of a hurricane seen from a great distance. There was something wrong, but the leader had no idea what, and in a voice of panic he shouted for his men, all of them, to open fire at the whirling sand that was growing wider, almost engulfing the trees now.

But nothing happened. The funnel was widening, moving away from the oasis and up the dune. The leader turned and began to struggle upwards, screaming over his shoulder for his men to follow. But those in the front rank had already been consumed by the sand. The last thing the leader remembered was his mouth, nose and ears filling with the stinging particles and then a weight, heavier than he'd ever felt, that slammed him into darkness.

When the sand began to rise, Mike had covered his head as best he could and rolled into a ball, shielding his face. He could hear shouts, then screams, but after a while it was silent except for the sound of the sand moving in the wind which slowly began to subside until he could feel the sun's heat once more. He was being lifted and a shower of water covered his face as his eyes jerked open.

"The bullet went through and out the other side of your arm. Very lucky." Jon Lee was leaning over him. His black hair was filled with sand and his body looked as if he'd taken the full force of the brief storm.

Mike sat up. The pain was sharp but he could live with it. "What happened?" He glanced up the dune and saw the bodies.

Jon Lee helped Mike get his shirt off. "Just something that happened long ago." He said no more as they stripped naked and bathed.

Mike's wound would require stitches but Jon Lee stopped the bleeding and bandaged it. No one else came over the dune. They thought they'd just missed the train to Mecca and would have to wait until evening because they didn't dare risk walking in the heat. But the inbound one was nearly an hour and a half late and the conductor, seeing Mike's condition, had let them board without a ticket or money.

Since the early heat wasn't so intense, the train didn't make the stop at the next water tower, and they were back in the city in less than an hour. It had been less than two hours since leaving the Holy City, and now they were riding through the city streets, hanging on the outside of an ancient bus that had twice the passengers it could carry. They reached the edge of town about three miles from the airport when tiles hitting here and there began to drop from the second floor of the shops along the crowded min-morning street.

"What's going on?" Mike asked, as people began jumping from the bus and running away as if the other occupants had the plague.

Andre had been half asleep on the couch in the plane's cabin when he was nearly tossed to the floor. He hurried to the cockpit. As he passed the open door, there was a crashing sound and he saw a portion of the hangar on the far side hitting the concrete. He pulled up the door and quickly fired up the engines. There was no time to warm up. He had to get out of there.

"Definitely an earthquake. Let's get off and get out and onto a side street so somebody doesn't bang into you." Mike was in pain so he couldn't move as fast, but they came out onto a side street, ducking tiles as they went. There was a series of trade shops on this street and one sold batteries, shoes, bicycles and mopeds. The owner had apparently gone upstairs to rescue his family. They jumped on a moped from the row parked on the sidewalk and rode precariously away, Mike hanging on as best he could.

They had no idea where they were going, but after several turns which they could only guess might lead to the airport, they were lost. A couple of policemen ran across in front of them and they nearly collided, but by saying "airport" several times and Jon Lee pretending he had wings, the police pointed to the east and they rode off. It was about three miles before the road gave way to a broader road lined with short, squat palm trees and in the distance to the right they saw the airport. One of the trees had already fallen in the road, and traffic was at a dead stop as the ground continued to shake. But they managed to skirt the horns and shouting along the dirt lip of the road.

When they got to the airport, they had no trouble finding the private hangars. Mike screamed. "He's pulling out, for God's sake! Wave at him!" Jon Lee took out his handkerchief and waved frantically as the plane turned slightly and taxied directly at them.

Andre had the ramp down in seconds and helped carry Mike up into the cabin and settle him on one of the leather couches. "What the hell were you doing, Andre?"

"Going airborne." He pointed towards the airport tower. It had broken in two and the top half was leaning against the bottom which was in flames. "Don't worry; I'd have landed again somehow. I wouldn't have left you. I was just going to ride this thing out. Cairo radio reported that it's an 8.7. This place has been bedlam. I saw a commercial liner disappear behind the terminal and then nothing but smoke." He raised the door and jumped back into the cockpit. "I've got to get us up." He was taxiing again, only much faster. "Do I repeat myself by exclaiming that this runway is about as well maintained as a California highway? Look at the ruts. When this thing ends, it'll be mostly rubble." He managed to dodge another commercial jet and passed four other large planes waiting to take off. As soon as the next one was airborne he butted into line and accelerated. They were up in seconds.

Andre let out a giant sigh and settled back in the seat. He looked over his shoulder at Jon Lee who was using the first aid kit on Mike's nasty wound. "I've never heard of a quake of this magnitude in this part of the world."

Jon Lee glanced up. "I don't think this was a quake, Andre."

Andre was quiet for several minutes getting the plane into the proper flight path as they crossed the Suez Canal again. Finally, he swiveled the chair around and looked at them. "Jon Lee?"

As he looked up from Mike's wound again, tears were streaming down Jon Lee's face. "They took their own karma, I guess."

11:20 p.m., Sunday, May 26h:
Downtown San Francisco

It had taken Designate 8 almost two and a half hours to get home. His clothes were soaked through with sweat, and he immediately grabbed the Cutty Sark and took a long sloppy drink. Jesus H. Christ! What had happened? He stumbled to the window but the city lights and night sky seemed unperturbed. He took another long pull on the bottle and could feel it working on him.

He didn't give a shit. "All fer nothin'" he said aloud. "Sweet Jesus! This ain't no world peace!" He nearly fell when the phone rang and he staggered over to pick it up. "Yeah?"

"Oh, my God, Mr. Mayor, it's a lunatic asylum down here! The press is camped out in the reception area and all down the stairs. Please, please, sir, you must come down right away!"

"Be there, I will…" he hung up and threw the phone to the floor. "Hell fire, this weren't no world peace! Crazy, bastards, crazy!"

It was then it struck him. He stood dead still in the middle of the floor. What about that thing in the Corfu Village garage? Esse had said it was the heart of the whole system from Canada down into Mexico, the main control for all of Sector 1. What if there was a quake? What if that insane kid of Esse's got his hand on the switch? What the hell would happen? That secret nuclear missile base up in Kennedy Meadows, just a short drive away? As he was going out the door in his dirty, wet and stinking three-piece suit, all he could think of was the doll's body that turned to steam as Panjali had nudged it into the swimming pool.

Epilogue

After the last had gone, the monk bathed. To the cook's excited questioning, he said nothing except that the warlord was defeated. When he had washed the battle away, he put on a fresh robe and went directly to the temple where he performed the rites as he always did, and the lighting of the incense and candles. At last, he settled in the lotus posture on a saffron pillow on the wood floor by the carved white granite statute of the Buddha and the fifteen statues depicting the Fifteen Steps of the Mastery of Zahu.

He was still there, silent and unmoving, three days later when the monks returned to the cook's baffling tale. What had happened to the boy? Had the cook become senile?

Their answer came as each in single file bowed and entered the temple. They felt it immediately, but stronger and stronger the closer they came to him: a sense of well-being so deep that the incense itself was permeated by an infinite tranquility. As each took a place near the young monk, they knew for the first time a radiance which until that moment had been only words in a chant.

The Abbot stood to one side. He rang the small copper bell which called them to mediation and vespers. It was normally the task of the youngest, the

293

boy who sat in blissful stillness before them. Kneeling, the Abbott prostrated himself before Wo Chin and remained so for a long time. When he rose, the bell tinkled like the echo of a very distant chime.

The Abbott spoke quietly, gazing in turn at each brother. "For the chronicles of Zahu, a bridge from the past has been rebuilt. A master who has gone beyond the 12th Circle has unfolded in our presence, traveling into and being our guide to the 13th, 14th and, finally, the 15th Circle of Mastery. Let us live within his grace and be as children to the voice and silence of his teachings."

Six months had passed since their return. Andre was still being Andre while the Arab world was just beginning to dig out from what many had called "a warning from God." Jon Lee had been terminated shortly after his hearing, but didn't appeal it. His course was set.

He leased his condo, moved into the Kiwan and though not yet in his heart, he assumed the role of master and took over the classes and duties of Yee Chin. He was as happy as he'd ever been, given the circumstances. Jon Lee would devote his life as his master had to opening the world to spirit through the grace of the body. Perhaps, though he thought of it without hope or anxiety, someday he would replace his master and attain—as Yee Chin had and as others before him had—15th Circle Mastery.

Mayor Joe Hennessey, Designate 8, had died of a massive heart attack in his office the night of the opening of the United Nations' *Week of Peace* celebrations. After an extensive investigation by the SID assisted by the FBI, the District Attorney had placed Charles Locke under indictment for bribery, money laundering and connections with organized crime. Finally, Police Chief McGrady had retired, but had been drafted to run for mayor of San Francisco; his vineyard would wait.

Mike put a down payment on five acres with a two-bedroom cabin just outside of Grass Valley, and was back on the investigative beat two to three days a week while still living at Anna's and writing an emotionally painful but partially healing book about the East Bay drug bust. Jon Lee had had dinner with him and Teri who had, as Mike put it, finally come up for a nightcap.

Those thoughts passed through him as he prepared to sit for his afternoon meditation in the temple. He kept a candle always lit for Yee Chin by his picture on the altar and another unlit, for Dama.

Forty minutes later he opened his eyes wide and stretched. The door to the temple moved slightly; it was probably the wind blowing the front doors ajar or a student come early for practice. He turned onto his knees, bowed deeply to the altar, rose and backed reverently from the temple.

He instantly sensed another's presence down the hallway by the entry doors. As he moved gracefully but cautiously toward the shadow silhouetted only by the expanding and contracting light from the windblown doors, the figure moved towards him. The person approached slowly, supported by a cane. He couldn't see the face because it was hooded from the light rain that had begun to fall earlier that day.

Jon Lee stopped and the cane stopped. "This is the Kiwan of Zahu. May I help you?"

They were about ten feet apart as the head turned slowly to face him, and one slim, delicate arm rose in response. The hood was lifted from the face and released, falling away to the shoulders where it rustled and lay still in the silence.

About the Author

 I took up writing when my parents told me I could not become a pickpocket. I gave up sending work to major publishers when the last agent who read one of my works (now on Amazon) told me it was an original action-adventure that could easily be converted to the screen, but he couldn't sell it. What? I have been blessed with two jobs I loved and love in my life: driving a cable car in San Francisco (gripman) and teaching junior college students who I still teach and still love and thank my good luck for the opportunity. I consider it an honor to have received advice from the late historian, Howard Zinn, and also from my wife and daughter. If you ever come up the coast from Los Angeles, don't stop in Santa Barbara where I live because we've got too many people here already.